THE HAWALA AGENT

THE HAWALA AGENT

SMARAK SWAIN

Srishti
PUBLISHERS & DISTRIBUTORS

Srishti Publishers & Distributors
A unit of AJR Publishing LLP
212A, Peacock Lane
Shahpur Jat, New Delhi – 110 049
editorial@srishtipublishers.com

First published by
Srishti Publishers & Distributors in 2022

10 9 8 7 6 5 4 3 2 1

This is a work of fiction. The characters, places, organisations and events described in this book are either a work of the author's imagination or have been used fictitiously. Any resemblance to people, living or dead, places, events, communities or organisations is purely coincidental.

To my sister, Smrutilekha.

This is for you, nani.

Acknowledgements

I thank all the officers and staff of the Income Tax department I have worked with in the twelve eventful years that I have been in the Indian Revenue Service. I also thank members of the community of tax practitioners – tax advocates and chartered accountants – who I have interacted with in the course of my duty as a public officer.

Together, tax officers and tax practitioners are some of the biggest gossipers in the country, and the source of many uncanny stories. Most stories about people with unaccounted wealth are raunchy and gossipy, so I have been a recipient of some of the most interesting gossips of our times. Some of these gossips have found their way as sub-plots in this story.

The primary plotline of this novel marries two different cases. First is the famous Jain Hawala Diaries case of 1991, in which a raid on Jain brothers led to seizure of diaries with sensational clues about large value hawala transactions. The Jain brothers were allegedly sending corruption money abroad and bringing money for funding terrorist activities in Kashmir, through the hawala route. Since money is not necessarily physically sent in a hawala transaction, if the allegations are true, then the money earned from corruption was redirected to Kashmir to fund terror activities. While all court cases pertaining to the Jain hawala diaries eventually collapsed and no one was convicted, the allegations of law enforcement agencies highlight an important modus operandi used in hawala finance.

The second case is of the discovery of a huge amount of cash and gold from an income tax raid in 2018 in Chennai. About 200 crore rupees and 105 kilograms of gold was seized from a contractor. Interestingly, this wealth was parked in houses of employees and two BMW cars! The idea of using these modus operandi to develop a plot came while interacting with my batch-mates in 62nd Batch of IRS. And I thank my batch-mates as well, for all their help.

I wrote a lion's share of the book while I and Ashima were under a pandemic-triggered lockdown in 2020. I thank Ashima for tolerating me through my long writing bouts, even though I was the only company within the confines of our house.

My gratitude to Hena Kumar Sukhna, IRS; Neeraj Agarwal, IRS; and Prateeti Goyal, IRS, for reading earlier editions of this book and giving their constructive feedback.

I thank my entire editing team at Srishti Publishers, and specifically Vini Bhati and Stuti, for putting in the extra effort to iron out the internal contradictions in the narration and bringing out the book in its present form. Arup and Jayanta Da have been my publishers and very good friends for more than five years now. I thank them both for their support and continued encouragement.

This is a work of fiction. Any views that could be purported to the author are entirely my personal views.

1

The Mystery of the Missing Wife

Nidhi Arora's first question when she called me was if I got fired for harassing a female subordinate.

I clarified that I was not fired. *I had resigned.* She kept baiting me, wondering why the #MeToo movement had not caught up with me yet. I had no choice but to point out that she was a cougar on the prowl; that young associates in her office should be warned about her. She did not find it amusing and drove to the point.

Deepak Bhide was in Mumbai and wanted to meet me. Apparently, he was in distress and needed help. Nidhi convinced, rather directed me to meet him.

Who Bhide? I wondered. *Oh, that Bhide!* I went down memory lane to recollect my experiences with him.

Bhide is not my friend. He was never my friend. We have not been in touch since graduation. We were not friends in college. Those days it was "uncool" to be friends with him. He was a dimwit (he still is!), but that should be no criteria to choose friends. And then, we were teens. We were unabashedly cruel and mean.

It was Thursday morning. The wife had left for office. I did not have a job. I had promised wifey that I would go out looking for a job.

Deep down, I knew that vendors do not sell jobs; not the kind of job I was looking for. I am skilled labour, after all. I cannot wander around sweatshops and construction sites, looking for a daily wage. I am a chartered accountant and a specialist in corporate espionage. They don't advertise such posts on job sites. But then, she is a neurotic woman. She could not tolerate me idling around the house all day.

If I *had* to get out, why not meet Bhide! Maybe I could have a couple of drinks at his expense.

▼

We met in a sports bar in Parel. As the bar was just opening up for the day, Bhide and I were the only crowd. He had swollen to double his size since college. At a height just below five feet, he looked like a penguin.

During our college days, I had found Bhide lacking in social skills. He was shy but spoke enthusiastically, like a kid, once he opened up to someone. After meeting him, I found that not much had changed about him.

We did small talk till the bartender came with my beer and his lemonade. After we received our drinks, there was an awkward silence. I could fathom that Bhide was troubled.

"I need your help," he said at last.

"What happened?" I asked.

"I… I… I don't know how to say this."

I tilted my head and feigned an expression of big-brotherly concern.

"My wife is gone."

"Cool!"

It is not always that a man could get rid of his wife. It called for a celebration. I was tempted to call for shots, but saw that Bhide was markedly perturbed.

I sat expectantly to hear his problem. But he became silent. I nudged him to speak freely.

"We are old friends. You can trust me."

"My wife has vanished. I need your help."

"With what?"

"With getting my wife back. Saswata Das has taken her."

"Saswata Das, as in *the* Saswata Das? The West Bengal Home Minister Das?" I asked out of sheer astonishment.

"Yes! That bastard has abducted my wife."

"Seriously? Why in the world would he…"

I stopped in the middle upon seeing his face contorted as if he was about to cry, but was not sure if he should. He was perhaps waiting for my permission to break down into a pool of tears. But then, maybe I am not the right person if one is looking for someone to empathize with his concern for a missing wife. I would feast for weeks if my wife vanished. Or voluntarily left.

But then, who am I fooling? She is never going to leave. After all, I stay in her house.

Bhide was excitable. He started saying a lot many things too fast. He ate away many words and sentences. So I encouraged him to try a drink. He preferred to have a glass of lemonade. He relaxed after taking a few gulps of lemonade and narrated all that had happened to him.

"We married. We were happy…" he started.

"You married and you were happy? Doesn't make sense. Tell me from the beginning. Who is she? How did you meet her? Take your time. Tell me all of it from the start."

"From the very start?"

"Yes, from the very start," I said, hoping he won't start from the day he came out of his mother's womb.

▼

Bhide's Story

After graduation, I moved out of the city and went to Bangalore. I know what you people thought about me. I was ridiculed and this affected my confidence. I was not sure if I could do Master's or if I could have a successful corporate career. My expectations were low.

So, I completed a professional course on handling SAP software and looked for a job. A distant uncle arranged a job for me in a software company. I handled the accounting side of SAP for this company.

The promoter of this company soon developed a liking for me. I am slow, I know that, but I am meticulous. I would report deviations of even a single rupee to him. Over time, I became close to him. He made me the head of the company's SAP business interface.

I was doing great professionally. So, my mother said I should marry and have a good wife. But it was difficult to find a suitable bride for me. After continuous efforts, my mother managed to find a sweet, homely girl. My marriage was fixed. After that I started talking with this girl over the phone. I developed feelings for her. For the first time in my life, I was getting the blissful feeling of falling in love. Everything was going good.

But the girl called off the wedding a few days before our engagement ceremony. First I thought, maybe she has an affair or something. But, she did not. The reason she gave for calling off the marriage devastated me.

Her parents told my parents that the girl was unable to develop romantic feelings for me. My parents could not understand what they meant by 'the feeling'. When they asked, her parents just said, *you know, the feeling. The feeling you get towards someone you marry.*

I could not understand what feeling they were referring to. So I called her and asked for an explanation. She said that she could never respect me and she could not marry a person she could not respect.

I felt very bad. I loved her. Then what was her problem?

My mother says I am very gentle at heart. The girl was unable to see my inner beauty. But she could not have done more damage to me. Not only did she break my heart, she made me loathe myself.

Jibes in college had bothered me, but never killed my spirit. However, this girl had killed my spirit. She drilled a hole inside me.

Slowly, I went into depression. My parents were staying in Mumbai and I was in Bangalore. I did not have friends in Bangalore. So the only people I met were at work. This increased my loneliness.

My only comfort in those days was food. There were good eateries near my office in Bangalore. I would munch on food all day while at work. Then, after coming back from work, I used to order delicious pizzas and burgers at home and eat.

I also developed a liking for online games. They were liberating for me as I could experiment with my perceived identity. I was the boring Deepak Bhide for the outside world, but inside the game, I was GladiatorTheGreat or NewBond009. The people I played with did not know my real name. They knew me by my screen name. I was good at both strategy games and shooter games. Very soon, I made a name for myself in gaming forums as GladiatorTheGreat and NewBond009.

Some of my online friends were nudging me to join Facebook games. These are multi-user games, which have become a big craze in recent years. Farm Heroes, Candy Crush and Criminal Cases had hogged too much of limelight for any gamer of some stature to ignore them. Initially, I was hesitant about joining Facebook. I knew that you get connected to the people of your past and present over Facebook. I did not have a particularly happy childhood or teenage years. Acquaintances of the past only reminded me of jibes and pranks they played on me.

But finally, I joined Facebook. My online status as an ace gamer – my *present* – weighed over my repulsion to my status among people in my *past*. Little did I know that Facebook would become a catalysing agent for the course of my *future*.

With time, I developed an addiction for Facebook. I would add any random person on my friend list, read all their posts and go through all album pics.

Facebook is a world in itself. Apparently, there is no one to judge you and yet, you are the object of social scrutiny. Regardless, there is always a perfect glow and incessant joy on your face. Your social standing is made up of simple things such as your status messages and your membership to some groups.

I started spending more time on Facebook. I would go through profiles of strangers and add those I found interesting. Mostly beautiful girls, to be frank! I also tried to hit on a few girls who had accepted my friend request. But somehow, I could not hit it off with any of them. Probably I did not have enough of 'chat charm'. And yet, I was not deterred by the unencouraging response. I kept adding new profiles and followed up on those girls who accepted my friend requests.

Then, something unfortunate happened to me. It was so bad that it took me days to come out of the trauma it caused me. I dreaded all those pleasant faces on Facebook after this incident. I realized that the faces on Facebook were masks that hid many dark-minded people. So I stopped sending friend requests.

▼

I listened to Bhide's tale intently. He took a long pause as he was overwhelmed with emotions

"What happened?" I asked.

What could have possibly happened over Facebook to make Bhide use the word 'trauma'?

"Let it be. It is not important for the problem I have come to consult you."

"I insist. Tell me what happened."

He was hesitant. I rubbed his arm, made a face like your mother makes when you catch a cold, and said, "Bhide, bro, you can trust me. I am here to help."

After taking a deep breath, Bhide continued.

▼

Bhide's Story

I had added a man who seemed to like gaming. These were usually men I thought I could interact with to enrich my knowledge. He went by the name Cool Dude Amo. He appeared to be a good-natured person. He was polite and funny to chat with.

Slowly, we hit it off well and ended up interacting for hours. We talked about girls, my job and gaming. He was like a therapist to me. I shared my apprehensions and complexes I had about myself. He was always there to listen to me patiently. He encouraged me to go to the gym and make a toned body and gave me ideas about personality building.

Gradually, we came closer, so I invited him to Bangalore. Amo accepted my invite. He said that his father has a cottage in the foothills of Nandi Hills and we could party there.

Excitedly, I went to the airport to receive Amo. He had come with another friend, a person he introduced as Tudo. Like Amo, he too seemed jolly and good-natured. What struck me about them was that they were both tall and athletic. They were wearing T-shirts, and boasted huge, toned biceps.

Amo had a Land Rover car waiting for him at the airport. We rolled into his car and directly went to Nandi Hills. We had some good time trekking in the hillside and then went to a nearby shack for drinks. Amo and Tudo had alcohol while I went for buttermilk.

Finally, we went to Amo's cottage. It was a beautiful property, luxurious and spacious. We went to our different rooms to freshen up. I came out to the dining hall to find Amo and Tudo already drinking. Amo talked at length about how he had planned the designs and collected many exotic whisky and vodka drinks from all around the world. He pestered me to try some wine from some famous vineyard in Italy, but I declined.

Then we went to the woods for a while. There, Tudo lifted me off the ground and swung me like I was a kid. I must admit, I liked it. These fellows were strong and muscular. At no point did they make fun of my short height or of how I speak or of how I look. I could be myself with them.

It seemed to me that both of them liked me too. Amo talked a lot about how my skin is soft and radiant. He said he was an astrologer and took my hand in his. He caressed my palm and said I am destined to have many lovers. Then, Tudo kissed me on the cheek. I did not know why he did that. But then, he had been behaving like a big brother all along. So I patted him on the back.

But, to my surprise, he became abrasive and tried to kiss me on the lips. It was awkward. I did not like it. In fact, I found it to be repulsive. I told him so. But he was unstoppable. He grabbed me by my shoulder and pushed himself into my mouth. I did not like it one bit. I tried to bite his tongue, which had burgled into my throat. He winced and slapped me hard across my face.

They forcibly undressed me and played with me. Then they undressed themselves. It was so horrible, looking at two naked men.

It became worse after this. They took turns and did bad things to me. I could not walk properly. They kept me in the cottage as a prisoner for days. Tudo had my mobile phone. He messaged my colleagues at work that I was sick and won't come for a few days. When my mother called, he messaged her that I was on a tour and shall call back when I return.

They used to beat me whenever I became violent. They forced me to wear colourful frocks and brassieres. But they were indulgent and delicate when they applied lipstick or eye gloss on me. I could not understand the dichotomy in their attitude towards me.

One day, Amo asked why I was in such a bad mood when I was being fed well and pampered.

"Pampered?" I shouted at him for all the bad things they were doing to me. Amo said that I would soon begin to enjoy it.

Then he called Tudo from the other room. They stripped in front of me. I winced the way a goat bleats when it realizes the butcher is about to knife him.

But, they did not come for me this time. This time, they kissed and played with each other. They became so engrossed in their act that they forgot about me. I silently slipped out of the cottage and ran.

I was not in a situation to walk, let alone run. Yet, I ran. I ran like my life depended on it. Amo and Tudo were so sick and twisted that I could not have survived in their captivity any longer.

▼

Poor Bhide! Bad things happen in this world to innocent people.

Bhide was still agitated by what happened to him in Amo's cottage. He shivered while he narrated his tragic tale. He was still perturbed. He seemed to have relived the trauma of violation of his modesty as he narrated the incident to me.

I raised my eyebrows, pressed my lower lip over my upper lip, and grimaced as if apologizing for what happened to him.

He said, "How can one human being treat another like this? And what gave them the right to force all this on me?"

"Amo and Tudo were perverts. Did you report the matter to the police?" I asked, even while I smirked involuntarily.

"No. I told all this to my mother. My parents immediately came over to Bangalore. My mother was kind and empathetic, but my father was irritated. He kept repeating that I need to grow up and act like a man. My mother suggested that we should report the matter to the police. But my father shouted at her. He said that what happened was shameful and we should drop it at that."

"Do you realize those two sodomite psychopaths are still on the prowl and may victimize other innocent people like you? You should have reported to the police," I said.

"Yes, I should have. I cannot tell you how much rage I have inside me for them. The pain of what Amo and Tudo did to me increased with every passing day. The imagery was vivid and nightmarish. I had gone into depression. If I could come out of the depression, it was only because of my mother.

"Unfortunately, they have vanished. Amo is not on Facebook now. Only after this incident I noted that all profiles in his friends list were of men. He does not have any girls in his connections at all. The profile he was using might have been a fake one. The profile was removed from Facebook within days of my escape. I tried to enquire from people in his friends list about him; but nobody knew him in person.

"I have made it the purpose of my life to take revenge on Amo and Tudo. I shall find out where they are and hunt them down," Bhide said. His jaws were clenched and fist had rolled into a ball.

"Have your lemonade, Bhide!" I said, "Do you want some ice?"

"I am alright," Bhide said. "Just got a little carried away."

He emptied the glass of lemonade in one gulp and wiped his lips with the back of his hand. "I have come to you with another matter that is serious and more pressing than this. I should not have gotten into this episode of my life," he said.

"Yes. Something has happened to your wife. Tell me about it," I said, hoping that he would take fewer digressions and come straight to the point.

Bhide continued.

▼

Bhide's Story

As I said, I again went into depression after the incident with Amo and his friend. I had to visit a therapist. I was making good progress there, healing my wounds. With time, it became almost tolerable for me and I returned to my old routine.

My therapist encouraged me to face my fears. I had discontinued using Facebook for some time then. It may sound odd to you, but social networking had become traumatic for me. I dreaded logging into Facebook.

But my therapist insisted that this was part of my therapy. I am grateful to him, for I would not have met the most amazing woman I know if it was not for my re-entry on Facebook. Her name was Swati Gupta.

Before the incident with Amo, I used to add members on Facebook indiscriminately. But I discontinued this habit during my second stint. Whatever time I spent online was on games and a few groups.

I had made a comment in one group and Swati messaged me referring to that comment, as she had a query on the subject. I messaged her back. We messaged for sometime and then she added me.

She did not have any pictures on her profile. She had limited friends, which made me apprehensive about her at first. But then, we exchanged numbers.

Swati is the most beautiful thing to have ever happened to me. I fell in love with her even before seeing her.

Honestly, there is nothing common between us. She has an MBA degree and worked for a recruitment company here in Mumbai. I am a graduate in commerce working in a software company. She is from Uttar Pradesh and based in Mumbai. I am a Maharashtrian based out of Bangalore. Yet, when we talked to each other, we did not realise how hours went by.

Love is the most wonderful thing to happen to a person.

With Swati I realized how blissful love is. I finally began to understand why love stories are celebrated in a grand way in books and movies. Swati came to Bangalore for a conference. That is when we first met. We met in a cafe near Cubbon Park. She had never shown me her photo. So I was not expecting much. Only unsure girls do not share their photo on such platforms. But as it turned out, she was an exception. She was gorgeous and classy. She had sharp, delicate features. Her nose was sharp, her lips abundantly pouty, and her eyes were large.

When we met, she complimented me on my looks. She said she loved my sense of humour. It was past afternoon and there was a moist breeze in the park. We held hands and walked for a while in the park. It was uncomfortable at first, as she is much taller than me. But she made me feel comfortable. She wrapped her arms around my shoulder and kissed me on my forehead. She said it is hard to find a good man with a good heart.

And then she invited me for dinner at the hotel where she was staying. It was the Chancery Pavilion on Residency Road. I got ready and reached the hotel at eight. She had asked me to meet her in her room. I reached her room and knocked at the door. She opened the door almost as soon as I knocked, as if she was waiting for my knock.

She was wearing a small, tight T-shirt over denim hot pants. The hot pants were extremely small and fit tightly on her. It appeared as though her fair, fleshy thighs forcibly sprouted out of the hot pants. She was so exposed that I felt shy. Although I blushed, she was comfortable in those pants. She asked me in and said she would need some time to get ready.

When she offered me wine, I said I don't drink. So she poured me orange juice from her minibar and made a glass of red wine for herself. She then came over and sat by me on the sofa.

Swati was an innocent girl. She did not understand that she was sitting inappropriately in my presence. And then, like a kid, she put a leg on me. She was so oblivious of the inappropriateness of this that it did not occur to her that I might have taken advantage of her. She was talking about some movie she had seen recently, but I was so shy I could not concentrate on what she was saying. There was also no way out for me as she had wrapped her arm around me.

The orange juice she offered was one of a kind. It made me dizzy. And light. I felt happy. I became talkative. We chatted for a long time. She planted kisses on my cheek intermittently. It felt good to be liked and kissed.

She said that she had so much wine that she felt hot. She took off her t-shirt and fanned herself. She was wearing just a bra beneath. Her things were meaty and abundant. I stared at them longingly.

But, I felt guilty that I was staring at them. I felt ashamed when I thought what she would think about me if she caught me ogling at her things.

So, I untangled myself from her and explained to her that this is a bad world. Men are not always good and they may take advantage of her innocence. So she should not expose herself so much in front of men.

She looked at me apprehensively and asked if I also intended to take advantage of her. I said that I am a man of honour –

maryada purush. These things in a girl should be seen after marriage and I would see these things after I marry her.

She was flummoxed when I told her about marriage. She said she just wanted to have fun. And then, I talked about marriage. I said that I love her and I wanted to marry her. I said if she had no problem, I would ask my parents to talk to her parents for her hand in marriage.

She became silent. Probably she did not want to marry me, I thought. Perhaps I was mistaken. She was so warm and loving all evening, I had thought that she was, maybe, interested in marrying me. I felt bad.

"I am not feeling well. I had a hectic day. I think I should rest," she said after a long, uncomfortable silence.

"You don't want to marry me?"

"No, no. It is not like that. I need time to think about it. Let's call it a day."

"Don't you want to have fun? We can play chess or watch some cartoon," I said. She laughed heartily. She said I was fun enough and she did not need anything else. She said she was indeed tired and needed to sleep. So I returned home.

Next morning, I phoned her many times, but she did not take my calls. I left numerous messages. She did not reply. I was crestfallen. Just when I had found the girl of my dreams, I had to confront the reality that she was not the girl of my dreams. I went to the Chancery Pavilion to meet her in person. But she had checked out of the hotel.

I understood that she was avoiding me. It was a wretched feeling of self-doubt, guilt and despair. After all the love and adulation she showered on me, she left me unceremoniously. I was devastated.

I stopped going to work. I did not get any motivation for my daily chores. I lay in bed gloomily all day long. I did not even feel like wallowing. My employer sent people to enquire after me. They tried to jolt me out of my gloom, but I was inconsolable. On their insistence, however, I agreed to visit the therapist again.

▼

Bhide's tragic tales might otherwise be unbearable, but were damn entertaining once I had downed five pints of beer.

Or was it six? Or seven? I don't know. I had lost count, and since Bhide was paying for it. Bhide's tragedies were giving me high in high noon that day.

I raised my hand to the bartender and signalled for another beer. I took a gulp of the chilled beer and asked Bhide to continue.

"She called me again after two months," Bhide said. "She wanted to meet."

"Why?"

"The same question came to my mind. I did not know why she wanted to meet me. But I was curious. I wanted to find out. Underlying this was also a desire to meet her and ask her why she left in the first place."

▼

Bhide's Story

So we met again, at the same café by Cubbon Park. I was there before her. I was naturally rude and edgy. I asked her as soon as she came and took a seat at my table, as to why she wanted to meet. She said she wanted to meet because she had missed me.

Given the pretext to the meeting, I thought she was mocking me. This added fuel to my anger and I said something I was to regret soon.

I said, "I have had enough of your smooth words and pretension. I know pretty well what kind of person you are. You are a cruel woman without a thought for others' feelings."

Her face fell on hearing this and I saw a shadow of sadness taking over her sweet demeanour. A tear rolled out from an eye and meandered down her fair cheek.

I had not expected this reaction from her. I realised that I was seeing her from a biased lens, owing to which I had missed out on something in her appearance that expressed distress and melancholy. She was wearing a white cotton shirt and black trousers. This is not how she had dressed the last time around she was in Bangalore. It occurred to me that there could be some reason for her sudden disappearance and lack of communication that I was not aware of.

"I cannot blame you for judging me. My disappearance was disrespectful and you are right in your place if you decide not to forgive me for that. But I had to go. The matter was so pressing that I had to go abruptly, without notice. You won't understand my predicament," Swati said.

By this time I was almost repenting having said those mean things to her. I apologised to her and pleaded for her to tell me what had happened that night in Hotel Chancery Pavilion. After some more requests and insistence from me, she explained her strange disappearance.

It turned out that she is the illegitimate daughter of Saswata Das, the home minister. He found solace in a relationship with a journalist with whom he had an illegitimate daughter. This daughter is Swati.

Swati said that her father is a mean person. He helped her get a good education, but never loved her. He always insisted that she refer to him as 'uncle', not 'father'. He was a public figure and image is everything in the public space. Once her mother was in a bad mood; she phoned him and threatened to speak to the media if he did not declare Swati as his daughter. She soon came to her senses and repented.

She died in a road accident two days later. Swati believes that her father got her killed.

A political associate by the name of Purnendu Mohalik was close to Das. He knew about Das's little secret. He had a fallout with Das in 2012, and Das kicked him out of his party. Ever since, Das has become insecure of the fact that Purnendu was privy to his secrets. He became paranoid that Purnendu may use Swati to expose him. These days, it is easy to determine lineage by a mere DNA test. Bringing Swati into the political stage would definitely mar his career.

Swati's mother had died back in 2004. She was living alone in Mumbai. Swati could feel tremors of what was happening in Kolkata in her small apartment in Mumbai. She indeed got calls from Purnendu Mohalik. But she avoided these calls. She knew that he was just trying to use her for political gains. She has no future in politics as an illegitimate daughter. She would only be maligning her father's name. So, she refused to set foot in the muck.

This, however, did not subside Saswata Das's paranoia. He hired a private agency and put her under surveillance. One evening she was returning from the office by local train. She realised that two strangers were following her. This spooked her. She strongly believes that Das had staged her mother's accident.

She did not know if he could get her eliminated too. Swati panicked and changed trains. She alighted at Victoria Terminus and took a train to Bangalore because she did not know who else to go to. So, she came to me.

She was underground when we first met. After I left her room at the hotel that night, she changed and went to the bakery. She spotted someone following her on her way to the lobby. She saw the same person trail her on her way back to her room. This frightened her and she left the hotel immediately. She ditched her phone, lest someone try to trace her using the SIM card, and boarded a train to Kochi.

▼

"This was why she had to leave abruptly," Bhide explained the reasons of Swati's disappearance.

"And you believed her?" I asked, surprised.

"Why wouldn't I?" Bhide asked.

I followed political stories and personalities fervently. I knew, for example, that Saswata Das had never married. He had a liberal education. He had no reason to hide a child if it was his. In fact, a daughter would help him politically. The daughter would be projected as his successor, which would bring stability to the party.

"Well, the thing about political personalities is that it is very easy to make stories around them. Being public figures, basic facts about them are available in the public domain. We know, for example, that Purnendu Mohalik was Das's strategist and they later had a fallout. You must ask for evidence when someone narrates such incredible stories."

Bhide must have been pretty lonely to befriend and trust a stranger on Facebook. And that too after the incident with Amo and Tudo. She had tried to seduce him – for whatever reason – and realised that he was an idiot. She did not have to take the pain to seduce him. Few words of affection and a cock-and-bull story would do the trick.

"I did not ask for evidence because I trust her. She would never lie to me. She is the basis of my faith. She is the basis of my existence. I love her. She loves me. Lawyers call for evidence, not soulmates."

"Look Deepak, we have seen enough of the world till now to know that anything can happen. I am not negating the possibility of her being Das's daughter. I am just sceptical about it. What happened then?"

"We got married."

"What do you mean you got married?" I asked,

"I mean we married. We had a wedding and then, we became man and wife," Bhide said, fanning his palm at my face. I saw a ring on his finger.

"My guess is that Das was not happy with your marriage," I speculated.

"No. He never got to know. Swati told me she could not go back to her job or her apartment, as Das's men were looking for her. We were in love and wanted to start a family. Things fell in place and we got married. We had a small private wedding. I did not inform my parents, as I have a huge family. My mother would have insisted on a large wedding and we did not want to attract attention. We discussed it and decided to inform my parents later. Just a few colleagues and my boss attended the wedding."

"When was the wedding, Deepak?"

"A few days after we met the second time. I think about a week later."

"Why was it so sudden?" I asked.

"It was not sudden. We were in love, and we understood each other. So we married."

"Did she go back to her job in Mumbai?"

"No. As I said, she had left Mumbai for good. I directly reported to the MD of my company and we were on good terms. On my request, my boss employed her in our company, Globosoft Chip Technologies Private Limited. She was made a deputy manager – HR in the company, a role much lower in corporate hierarchy than her experience would land. She is both intelligent and hardworking. Her experience was soon spotted and the boss made her his personal secretary."

"Then, how did she vanish?" I asked in a serious tone. To my question, Bhide continued his dramatic story.

▼

Bhide's Story

She was *kidnapped*.

A part of her job profile as PS to the MD was to travel a lot. She had to go to Hyderabad and Mumbai to handle meetings of the board of directors, asset acquisition, compliances with registrar of companies, RBI and SEBI. She had gone to Mumbai two days before her disappearance.

It was 5 April. She left home at 8 a.m. for the airport. She had a flight to Mumbai at 10:00 a.m. I was in constant touch with her over the phone while she was in Mumbai. After two days, on 7 April, I spoke with her in the morning. But I could not reach her cell when I phoned in the afternoon. Her WhatsApp was also not working. I got a bad feeling that something had happened to her.

When I did not receive any information from her till late evening, I called a liaison officer of my company in Mumbai. He said he had not met Swati anytime in the last two days. Swati had gone to Mumbai to file some paperwork and the liaison officer should have ideally helped her. I called my boss, N. Anbu Selvam. He was also in Mumbai, but he sounded busy. He said he was not in touch with Swati.

By evening, I was distressed. A colleague suggested I should immediately file a complaint with the local police. She offered to accompany me to the police station. We were leaving the office premises when I got a call from my boss asking me about Swati. I said that Swati was out of reach since morning and that I was going to the police station to report it.

Boss was in an unusually bad mood. He asked me not to go to the police. He said he had sent a person to Swati's hotel. He assured me that he would find Swati, but I should not approach the police in any case. I shouldn't worry and go home. I had premonitions that something bad had happened to Swati. I wondered if Saswata Das might have kidnapped her.

Early next morning, there were impatient knocks on the door. I opened the door. Palani Kumar, head of security at

Globosoft, barged in. He was followed by few other men wearing Globosoft's security uniform. Palani's men spread out into different rooms and searched the rooms thoroughly, in the process ransacking the whole house.

I got hold of Palani and asked him to explain the meaning of all this. Rather than answering my question, he asked me to spill out everything I knew about Swati."

"Basically you know nothing about this girl you married," he shouted after I answered to him. His aggressive behaviour surprised me.

"You met her on Facebook and fell in love. She told you a cock-and-bull story about her lineage and that was enough for you. Let me tell you, she is a ghost! She is a fucking imposter."

I did not like his tone or his swearing at my wife. The way he talked infuriated me. I told him to talk respectfully about my wife. He said, "Your wife? What wife? What's her name? Tell me, what's her name? There is no one by the name Swati Gupta. Her PAN card and driving license are forged. The PAN number she quoted in her resume is of a man who died years ago. We went through the records she submitted with HR. She never worked in the company in Mumbai she claims she worked for. Her Mumbai address does not exist. We let an imposter into our organisation and now she has messed with us."

"It can't be," I said. I was confused.

"Oh yes, it is. You know what? You are responsible for this security lapse. It all happened because the boss patronised you, you dimwit. He should have known better."

I tried to engage Palani in a conversation, but he was too irritable to talk to me. I silently looked on while his men rummaged my house. They did not find whatever they were looking for. Palani asked them to leave the house, and then turned towards me. He had regained his cool by then.

"Look Bhide, we go way back. I know you. I know you are a good man. You are a gem of a person. But your innocence may put me in trouble. Help me, please. But first understand me. The girl who came to you as 'Swati Gupta' is an imposter. She had come here to take advantage of you. Everyone who had attended your wedding was wondering why that girl married you. You two are a mismatched couple. She is tall, smart and stunningly beautiful. We could see the contradictions; still no one even imagined it could be a set up. She used you to enter Globosoft. You being a loyal employee, the boss employed her without screening her profile. We screen every profile and do background checks on each newcomer in the company. We did not do it for her. She effortlessly joined the inner coterie of the company. And now she has vanished without a trace."

"But it does not make sense. I love her. She loves me. This is how marriages work. We are happy with each other," I reasoned.

"You *were* happy with her," Palani said. "She was pretending all along. Trust me boy, she has run away."

"There must be an explanation. She was on the run when we met. She might have changed her identity then. She has not run away. Saswata Das's men must have found her and kidnapped her. We need to report this to the police."

"No police!" Palani said. "Do not involve the police. We are trying to find her. This is the MD's instruction. We won't involve the police. If Das is behind this, police cannot help. You cannot expect policemen's help when you accuse the home minster of a state of kidnapping and criminal conspiracy. They will only do more damage. Police will find the forged PAN and driving license she submitted in our office. Police will file a fraud case against her. If you love her, would you allow the police to book her for fraud? You need to trust us on this. I have my men looking for her. The MD has promised to take professional assistance in tracking her. But we will not go to the police."

What Palani said made sense. I had zero conviction in Palani's accusations that she was an imposter. How could she be? She married me in person. So what if Swati Gupta is not her name? It was *she* who I married. We followed the holy rituals of marriage. We were living happily. We enjoyed each other's company. This turn of events came out of the blue. She is in some deep trouble. I did not want to further aggravate the situation. So I agreed not to approach the police. Palani promised to keep me updated on the search for Swati.

▼

"Why was Palani so agitated? Your wife vanished, not his. And what were his men searching for in your house?" I said, after patiently listening to Bhide's sob story.

"I asked Palani about it. Palani said that admitting Swati into Globosoft was a big security breach. Swati was PS to the MD and so was privy to many confidential management decisions. Management has been working on taking the company public and issuing IPO. Swati handled most compliance documents related to the IPO issue. Swati had been made the company's authorised representative in SEBI. She has signed on many government forms on behalf of Globosoft group. When the company people found that her identity cards were forged, they were stunned. So boss sent Palani to my residence to see if she had kept any confidential documents at home. They do not know why she vanished. The theory in our office is that she might be a corporate spy employed by a competitor company."

I now understood why Nidhi referred Bhide to me. It is possible that Swati Gupta is a corporate spy, but improbable. A corporate spy would not leave evidence that could implicate her. Her forged documents were in Globosoft's office records. It would be easy to trace her and take legal action. It cannot also be a case of insider trading, since the company hadn't yet gone public. Whatever the case, Bhide had my attention now.

"My guess is your company's personnel have failed to find her," I said.

"I have no clue what is happening. I was immediately transferred to the Chennai office. I don't know what they are doing, but they have not found her. I do know what has happened. Saswata Das has kidnapped her. Officials at Globosoft find it difficult to believe that she is his illegitimate daughter. But everything falls in place once you accept this fact," he stopped to catch his breath, but continued again soon after.

"There is another possibility. Perhaps the Globosoft management is hand-in-gloves with Das. They may be tricking me. Suspecting this to be the case here, I finally went to the Domlur police station last week. The station head officer did not register the FIR. He asked me for evidence that I actually have a wife. I showed him photos of our wedding. He said I was posing with a model. I could not understand. But pretty soon, Palani walked into the police station. The SHO explained to me that *I* was missing for days and Palani had sent a lookout request for me to the SHO! The SHO said he had a detailed discussion with my therapist on my condition. He understands that I suffer from PTSD (Post-traumatic Stress Disorder). He suggested I return to my therapist for professional help.

"Palani grabbed me by my collar once I was outside the police station. He warned me against causing any more nuisance. He said that my therapist has certified that I am schizophrenic. Police believe I should be admitted to a hospital. Then he said, pretty menacingly, that I would be sent to the mental ward if I set foot in the police station again."

I had not considered this angle. Had Bhide indeed lost his mind? Everything he said would instantly make sense if he were considered schizophrenic.

"Do you have a photo of her?"

Bhide nodded and showed me a few photographs on his phone. The woman was a stunner – fair, with sharp features, pouty lips and big eyes. It was difficult to digest that a woman with such looks would fall for Bhide.

"Okay. So what help do you want from me?" I said.

"I want you to find her. Nidhi said you are an ace detective."

"She has misled you. I am a chartered accountant, as you pretty well know," I asserted.

"But she said you used to do spying for big companies."

"Yes, I specialise in forensic audit. My work requires domain expertise in accounting. But yours is a kidnapping case. It should be dealt by a detective."

"Then at least find me news of any involvement of Globosoft. These private detectives in India are small timers only. All they do is background check on potential grooms and brides. They wouldn't understand how corporates work. Nidhi said that you are good at investigating. You were fired by your company, so you have plenty of free time."

"I was *not* fired," I said, at a somewhat high decibel. "I had a difference of opinion with the management. I quit."

"But you do have lots of free time, don't you?"

I shrugged. It is true, I was fired. It is true that I have lots of free time. I realised there was no reason for me not to dabble in this intriguing tale narrated by Bhide.

"Alright, I will do some preliminary research and let you know my opinion. Send the pictures of your wife to me on WhatsApp. Also give me a list of personal effects left behind by your wife. Did she leave a diary or note behind?"

Bhide replied in the negative.

"Which hotel did she stay in during her visit to Mumbai?"

"She stayed at the Apollo Green hotel. It is in Colaba, close to the Gateway of India."

"A tourist destination, huh? Do all company employees stay there when on tour? Usually companies have corporate tie-ups with some hotels," I asked to get more clarity.

"Yes. The boss stays at The Royale. He conducts business dealings at the Royale, and Apollo Green is a three-star property near it. So other employees stay at Apollo Green."

Bhide's response got me thinking.

2

The Hawala System

"… Compulsory Convertible Debenture or CCD in short, is a hybrid financial instrument. CCDs are, at the same time, both debt and equity. An Indian company that takes CCD from a foreign investor has to pay an interest on it. In this way it is a debt instrument. However, CCD agreements contain a clause by which the CCD owner has an option to convert it into shares at a predetermined ratio," Saby Biswas explained to the class.

He scribbled over a diagram of a corporate structure he had drawn on the black board and looked back at the class. All he could see was blank faces.

There was pin-drop silence in the class, which he had misunderstood as deep interest. He could now see that no one really followed what he was saying; the silence was part of the discipline inculcated in the rigorous training programme.

"Any doubts?" Saby Biswas asked. Blank faces!

Saby Biswas had been invited to take a class on FEMA*

---

* Foreign Exchange Management Act.

laws at a training session of National Investigation Agency (NIA) officials. NIA is the country's nodal agency on anti-terror operations. NIA sleuths are recruited from police forces and cannot be expected to understand the basics of finance, let alone the complex subject of corporate finance. Biswas changed tact and tried to focus on the utility of foreign exchange laws for an anti-terror agency.

"How do you plan and execute cross-border acts of terror?"

Before anyone could venture a guess, he continued, "You need significant resources on the ground to successfully execute a terror attack. You need men on the ground to conduct recce. You need to gather intelligence on movement of people and security persons in the area you wish to strike. You need dedicated sleeper cells to collect such intelligence. You need logistical support to collect arms, ammunition and bombs. Finally, you need support of local sympathisers so as to escape the intelligence grid of the host country. All this costs a lot of money. Which means you have to move a lot of money across the border into the host country.

"A counter-intelligence strategy could be to detect terror financing and stop it. That is, choke the veins of a terror network. If you block funds meant for running a terror network, you can disrupt the entire network without shedding a drop of blood.

"Now, bringing funds into India is not all that easy. RBI regulates and monitors all cross-border financial transactions. Any foreign donation is audited under the Foreign Contribution Regulation Act or FCRA. So terror financiers use front businesses and colour their money as legitimate business. And then, there are some illegal channels of getting money into India. To appreciate the complexities involved in both legal and illegal channels, every counter-terrorism team should understand foreign exchange rules of the country."

"What are the illegal channels?" someone asked from the back benches. Saby could see curiosity in the eyes of these trainees. Without the heavy jargon and terms of finance, they could now relate to the lecture.

"There are two preferred illegal channels – Hawala and physical smuggling of counterfeit currency. Smuggling of counterfeit currency in Indian rupees serves dual purpose. The expense incurred by the terror-patron is low, since counterfeit notes are cheaper than real notes. Secondly, counterfeits destabilise our monetary system. Physical smuggling usually happens through the porous Nepal and Bangladesh borders, and is fraught with risks of getting caught. So, Hawala remains the most preferred illegal channel to bring terror funds into India."

"Why cannot law enforcement agencies ban Hawala, sir?" asked a student.

"Because it is sacred to Muhammedans. Banning it will hinder their religious independence," said another.

"Who said? I am a Muhammadan. There is no such thing sacred to my religion," said the third student.

"How will you ban it? In Hawala, you show a ten-rupee note to a person. If it is the right note, the agent gives you money. How can it be banned?" quipped a fourth.

And then, the class disintegrated into disorganised chatter as the trainees discussed animatedly about Hawala.

Saby wondered how these trainees, with years of law enforcement experience in the field, could be so prejudiced and so uninformed about Hawala. He slapped the duster against a tabletop to draw the class's attention.

"I am afraid your understanding of Hawala is severely lacking. It's a very simple process. At the same time, its execution can be pretty complex. First let me clarify that it has nothing to do with Islam. Hawala has been practised for thousands of years in India. In fact, Hindu traders used Hawala more efficiently than Arabic traders. Large family farms developed in medieval India due to the appropriate usage of Hawala as a financial instrument. Even today, the largest Hawaladars of India hail from certain Hindu and Jain castes."

There was absolute silence in the class. As he received the unwavering attention of his students, he continued.

"Hawala is a subject close to my heart. If you stay patient, I can explain the origin and development of Hawala over the ages. Let me begin at the very beginning.

"Hawala is a simple process of money transfer. Say, your brother is studying in America and you want to transfer some money to him. You give some money to a Hawaladar in your neighbourhood (let's call him H_I). His associate in America (H_A) pays your brother in dollars. The transfer takes place without physical movement of money. Hawaladars settle their running accounts once a year. This is the basic logic behind any Hawala transaction.

"The functions performed by Hawala can be performed by any formal system too. However, formal systems are not as quick as Hawala. Funds transferred from one country to another are sent to clearing houses and exchange bourses and finally reach the bank of the recipient. The commission charged by banks for small value fund transfers is high.

"The Hawala system works on trust. That's why Hawala is often referred to in Western press as an honour system. You cannot claim damages or file complaints with the law if your money does not reach your brother in America. Yet money always reaches your brother. There has to be trust between a client and Hawaladar. There has to be trust between Hawaladars at source point and destination. Usually these two Hawaladars are members of the same family or of a close-knit community.

"So you see, Hawala is purely a money remittance system. Hawala is not a bad system in itself. Nor is it a channel for money laundering. Main problem with Hawala is that you cannot establish a *money trail* in it. That's why all kinds of illegal trades depend on Hawala for fund movement.

"All transactions in a Hawala route are in cash. The Hawaladar does not maintain KYC norms. A drug dealer in India may go to a Hawaladar and ask him to transfer funds to his supplier in Thailand. The Hawaladar would not know whose money he is dealing with. Nor does he maintain proper accounts. The Hawaladar only keeps track of his debit/credit with other Hawaladars which he settles once a month or year, depending on the number of transactions.

"Along with the formal economy that is accounted for, there is a parallel economy, a black economy that runs underground. The trades happening in the parallel economy are not recorded in any bill or *challan*. The money earned and expensed in this parallel economy is not reported to the tax authority. It happens underground. You can visualise this parallel economy like this

– a builder receives payment for land sale partly in cheque and partly in cash. He reports the transaction in cheque but does not report the transaction in cash. Cash received by him is part of the parallel economy. It does not figure in his books.

"A wrong government official at the right place at the right time gets kickbacks for misusing their power. They cannot declare this kickback in their income tax return. This becomes part of the parallel economy. Think about human traffickers, organs and human parts traders, drug traffickers, poachers – they trade continuously through established trade routes, illegally. These trades happen underground. The cash generated from these illegal businesses becomes part of the parallel economy.

"Hawaladars are like the arteries and veins of this parallel economy. What banks are for the formal economy, Hawaladars are for the parallel economy."

As the class was engrossed in his explanation, Saby gave a content smile. At six feet and two inches, he looked imposing. However, being uber stylish, he always sported a goatee and long mane that he had knotted into a ponytail. He was wearing jeans and a printed T-shirt, which some would consider out of place in a formal classroom.

He had worried before the class that he may not have the trainees' full attention. But they all looked serious and solemn now. He had their attention.

To summarize, he said, "Hawala can sound very simple to you. The logic of Hawala is pretty simple. It is money transfer from one place to another without filling up a form. Practical implementation of Hawala is where the complexity arises.

Implementation of a Hawala network is not possible without trust among members of the network.

"If an American or a French citizen wants to start a Hawala network in their country, they won't be able to. Because today's French society or American society is an individualistic society. Social pressure on an individual is low. Two individuals, even kins, would not trust each other with money and business without a formal contract."

Biswas was satisfied. The class was reasonably enthused, although a few trainees still looked bewildered. They would naturally relate to the lecture when he comes to black money, drug money and blood money.

3

The First Breakthrough

Back home, I recollected Bhide's narration in my mind. I did not have sufficient facts to reach at a conclusion, or even a hypothesis about what actually happened.

First, I had to eliminate possible theories with low probability. For instance, could Bhide's wife be the illegitimate daughter of a minister? There was no way of proving or disproving it. I could not walk into the minister's house and make enquiries. It sounded so improbable that I took the risk of eliminating it upfront.

Next, could Bhide be schizophrenic? Could all of this be a figment of his imagination? This is quite probable. Two men raped him. Rape is the biggest violation of one's dignity and self-image. The trauma resulting from a rape could spiral into any sort of mental disorder, including schizophrenia.

I had developed contacts with resourceful persons of the hospitality sector during my days with Pharmabus. I have humoured many with drinks and cricket passes. I phoned Thuingmang, an event manager from Manipur, and asked him to verify if Swati Gupta had checked into Apollo Green or The Royale on 5 April 2018.

To my sheer luck, he said that he could get the information in an hour. I disconnected and tried to phone Saby Biswas, a close friend and a former colleague. He was a consultant in the corporate communication division of Pharmabus when I was employed there. He maintains quid pro quo with every major law enforcement agency of the country, by feeding them with market intelligence. I wanted to run this girl's photo by him. But Saby Biswas cut the call and messaged that he was in a class.

I buzzed Nidhi over IM to which she immediately replied.

Nidhi: Digyen Burmah?

Me: That's right, Nidhi. I buzzed you about Bhide. I met him today. Why did you send Bhide to me?

Nidhi: For old times' sake. Plus you have some time ever since you were fired.

Me: I quit.

Nidhi: Ya ya ☺

Me: I did not know you were close to Bhide.

Nidhi: No I was not. Poor fellow, everyone was so unkind to him he was almost a loner in college. He suffered through all of that.

Nidhi: Digyen we have to help him. He is distressed.

Me: Bhide told me he has already narrated his story to you.

Nidhi: Yes.

Me: What do you think happened to his wife?

Nidhi: What do you think happened?

Me: They are a mismatched couple. I saw the wife's pics. The Easy Prey law states that colleagues at work claw upon the woman whose husband is a hussy. That silly Bhide could not control the bombshell, and he let her go on frequent tours to other cities.

Nidhi: So?

Me: Someone in office was banging his wife.

Nidhi: Extramarital? They were deep in love.

Me: You kidding me? Bhide is madly in love. We can't say the same for his wife.

Nidhi: They were both in love . It is difficult for you to appreciate love between a stunner and an average looking man. Because your definition of love is skin-deep. You confuse love with attraction. You have never felt love deep down, so such a love is only fiction to you.

I don't know why women find me an easy target to lecture on love. And why they accuse me of not understanding love.

Nidhi: Now that I think about it, Bhide's wife was madly in love with him.

Nidhi: The company people are playing tricks. I smell corporate muck. That's why I sent him to you. You need to take up the case. You have worked for big corporates and spied on other corporates. You know how to handle their bullies.

Me: And I have lots of free time. Right?

Nidhi: Move to Bangalore for a while. Bhide has done well for himself and is ready to spend a chunk of his savings to find his wife. Also, you may get some of me at Bangalore.
Me: Get some of you after you have spilled yourself all over me all these years? And this is supposed to be a perk?
Nidhi: ☹
Me: I think I will work on the case.
Nidhi: ☺

▼

Mang called me in less than an hour.

"No one by the name of Swati Gupta checked into Apollo Green on 5 April or 6 April. I queried with the Royale hotel too. Apparently they have many secrecy norms, due to which it was difficult for employees to get access to guest lists. At last, I had to call the hospitality manager. Swati Gupta's name is not in the guest list of the Royale for 5 April or 6 April. But man, here is the scoop! The hospitality manager at the Royale knows her. She was in the Royale on 5 April. She has checked into the Royale many times earlier with her husband, N. Anbu Selvam. He being a regular guest, the hospitality manager personally deals with the couple. Anbu Selvam had taken a room on 3 April and Swati Gupta had joined him on 5 April. That's why her name does not appear in the guest list."

I let out a whistle.

"Did you get what you were looking for?" Mang said.

"Somewhat!"

"Swati Gupta is not Anbu's real wife?" he asked.

"Kinda!" I said.

"His real wife wants divorce and an alimony handful? And now has evidence of his infidelity?" he raced his imagination.

"Even if she does not, there is evidence now," I said.

"Oh man!" Mang said gleefully.

"Mang, I need you to get me CCTV footage of this girl in the Royale on 5 April and later. I also need CCTV footage of Anbu Selvam from 3 April till the date he checks out."

"Now that's difficult. I will have to get to the security guy and..."

"My client will make payments for it," I said confidently.

"How much?"

"Expenses, bribes and a mark-up!"

"Okay man, I think it can be done," he said and hung up.

I was tempted to call Nidhi and give her the news, so she could have you-don't-understand-love blown all over her face. I would have, at the moment, had Biswas da not phoned.

"Biswas da, need some help."

"Shoot."

"I am in the middle of an investigation. A guy was chatting with a girl over facebook. I need to trace the girl. I have the IDs and chat records... can we use them to track the girl?"

"Finding a trail over Facebook would be difficult. They have multiple firewalls and their codes are impenetrable."

"Come on da, you know the right men to get the work done. It is not asking for much," I said, trying to persuade him.

"Yes, it is asking for much. No hacker would try to go through Facebook's server from a proxy server in India. It would be asking for too much trouble. Besides, the hacker would leave his own trace while sniffing through the chat trail. They have to set up a dummy server in Russia and route access through it. Russian hackers have developed fine Trojans to pass firewalls without getting noticed. But for this, they need to identify the right Russian hacker and take his help, Trust me, the costs are prohibitive," Biswas blabbered.

"How much time are we talking about here?" I asked restlessly.

"May be a month. May be more."

I would crack the case in less than a month.

"Okay. Forget it. You have a contact in IB, don't you?"

"Who said so?"

"Chinese whispers, da."

We had a good rapport back in the days we worked for Pharmabus. I knew Saby Biswas would go out of the way to help me.

"Da, this contact of yours has access to all intelligence databases maintained by IB. IB has made a compilation of all IDs formally registered with various wings of the government. The database has details of Aadhaar cards, driving licenses, PAN, voter IDs, passports and any other data they could lay their hands on. Da, I need you to run this girl's picture on IB's database. It may be an easy way to know her identity."

"That database is to identify criminals and terrorists," he informed.

"This girl is probably one. I am onto something here. Please da."

"Hmm, send me the photo. Also a brief on the probable age group. I cannot commit anything now," he said.

"Another thing! Can you get me call detail records of a few phone numbers with tower location details?"

"That's illegal. Service providers would not entertain such a request."

"But you did manage to get those multiple times. Call records are accessible to most intelligence and investigation wings. You can procure through them."

"I will see what I can do."

"Thanks da. I owe you."

I said that I would email the details to him and hung up. Thereafter I opened my laptop and downloaded audit reports of Globosoft and its sister concerns from the website of the Ministry of Corporate Affairs. I also looked up a flight to Bangalore.

I heard some activity from the patio and knew Sneha, my wife, was back from office. She came into the drawing room and placed her sandals on the shoe stand. She greeted me with a warm smile (the kind of smile that had deceived me about her in the first place), came over and placed an arm on my shoulder. She peeped into my laptop and her brows furrowed.

"Are you going to Bangalore tomorrow? Were you even planning to tell me about it? Why are you going to Bangalore? The flight is at six in the morning. Digyen, sometimes I feel we are strangers sharing a house. You don't even tell me what you are up to. I have been forwarding you so many job openings. How many job interviews have you attended? I am killing myself caring about you and you are going to Bangalore! Why are you going to Bangalore? Or are you going on a holiday? Who are you meeting in Bangalore?" Sneha said and paused for breath.

Sometimes I think Sneha speaks faster than she thinks. I told her that I was hired by a corporate group, as it sounded nice. Being hired by an old classmate to find his wife would not sound hi-fi to Sneha.

Sneha's face instantly brightened. For the rest of the evening, she fluttered around the kitchen and dining space cheerfully, like a mouse.

Later, she came to bed after dinner in a flunky new nightdress and I knew the girl was ready for some heat. Sneha is a feisty and heavy woman, with a milk-fair complexion and abundant curves. I actually prefer disrobing her from a sari than a nightdress. But I wasn't complaining; about a month after the Pharmabus incident, she turned frigid, and denied any sex, making it an implicit bargain against me getting gainfully employed.

I grabbed her, pulled her to me, and aimed for her lips. But before I could get into her throat, she asked, "What is the case about?"

"They want me to find a missing employee. The employee is another employee's wife and she has gone missing," I said.

"Oh!" she looked at me surprised. "This sounds like a criminal case. Why would they need a corporate fraud specialist? Why wouldn't they ask the police to do the job?"

"They do not want to involve the police. They probably did not go to a private detective because the husband is a friend. He studied with me in grad school."

"Hmm okay!" she said. "Honey, can you take care of yourself in Bangalore?"

"I won't be in Bangalore for more than a week," I said.

▼

I boarded the flight to Bangalore.

During my flight, I studied the background of the company and transferred some Globosoft accounts figures to an Excel sheet.

Globosoft Chip Technologies Pvt Ltd is a privately held engineering design company registered with Chennai's Registrar of Companies. It uses automation software to design circuits that can be embedded into chips.

Directors of the company are N. Anbu Selvam, N. Shashi Selvam, and Roopalaxmi Sivanarayanan (wife of Anbu Selvam). Anbu Selvam is the Managing Director. These three directors own, among themselves, ninety-five percent of shares of the company.

The company had an annual turnover of four hundred odd crores in the financial year starting 1 April 2016 and ending on 31 March 2017 (FY 2015-16). There are few subsidiaries, but with minimal business activity.

Roopalaxmi Sivanarayanan led a charitable organisation by the name of Malabar Children Education Society. The trust got almost hundred crore rupees of foreign donations yearly, but the same had tapered down, FY 2014-15 onwards.

I observed that this coincided with a new government taking charge in Delhi in May 2014. The new government tightened the screening process for foreign donations into Indian trusts under the Foreign Contribution Regulation Act (FCRA).

Globosoft specialises in simulation and design of Integrated Circuits (IC). ICs compress complex electronic functions in a single small plate called the 'chip'. Rise of IC chips has revolutionised the world of electronics. Before the advent of

IC technology, we had televisions which were similar to the size of a cabinet. Now we have LCD and LED televisions that look smaller, yet give much better picture quality. Moreover, electronic devices are becoming smaller and smaller every day. For instance, mobile phones have given way to smartphones of the same size.

M/s. Globosoft Chip Technologies Pvt Ltd is a contractor for chip developers. Electronics companies based in Western countries outsource a part of simulation programming and testing to developing countries like India. There are many reasons for this. India is a country of cows and engineers. I can throw a stone at a crowd in a traffic junction, or a political rally, or a village haat, or a nude beach carnival (if there is one), or a railway platform and have a probability of nine in ten to hit an engineer or a bovine. Naturally, engineers come cheap in India. They are nine times cheaper than an engineer in the USA. If you throw a burger at an Indian engineer and call it a bonus, he will appreciatively wag a tail and slog the weekend too.

But the outsourcing market for chip testing is not as straightforward as the outsourcing market for software coding. MNCs cannot compromise with quality in R&D. That's why they contract out their simulation process, only to such companies that have established a reputation in academia and research. Globosoft is a favourite R&D contractor of MNCs in India. It boasts of contracts from likes of Texas Instruments, Sony, Nokia, Apple on its website.

But after browsing through trade sites and technical forums, I understood that Globosoft used a strategy called *landscape capturing* to win the confidence of MNCs. In landscape capturing, a new company in a new area bombards the market with research papers and patents. The patents may not be commercially viable; the patents may not be any remarkable invention over technologies already available; the research papers may be purely literature surveys, or results of running old algorithms on new platforms. What matters is quantity.

Globosoft Chip has a whopping 429 patent applications based on inventions by its employees, and 123 of these have been awarded patents. Of these, a total of 0 patents have been commercially harnessed. Yet, the strategy has worked and its turnover has steadily jumped over the years from two crore in FY 2008-09, its year of inception. The way the company has gained credibility among academic snobs and posturing scientists impressed me, especially given the fact that the founders, Anbu Selvam and Shashi Selvam, are both graduates in political science!

During my analysis, I found that while the sales turnover of the company has increased by leaps and bounds, its net profit margin has remained consistently low, earning before interest and taxes of less than 1% of total turnover.

The field is technology-driven and attracts both cheap capital and high returns. Profits in the service sector vary between 10% and 30% turnover. Profitability can go up to 50% of turnover for outsourced contracts from Western countries. Profitability in research & development services and niche technical testing can go up to 60%. On the contrary, this company has abnormally low profitability. Consistently low profits do not make business sense, given the meteoric rise in turnover over the years. The purpose of any business, after all, is to make profits.

So, *why is it consistently bleeding?* In spite of huge expansion in turnover over the years, it is not making profit. My instant conjecture was that the company was perhaps under-reporting its profits to save on taxes. Then I analysed the line items of the company's business expenses. It outsourced most of its work to local software companies. US-based chip making companies contracted testing work to Globosoft. Globosoft further sub-contracted the work to domestic companies.

Naturally, it would make only a modest profit margin.

But then, why would it take the pain of applying for patents if it is actually not performing any business activity?

4

The Confrontation

Bhide phoned me minutes after my arrival in Bangalore and enquired after me. I assured him that I have already made a breakthrough, without disclosing the bit about Anbu Selvam nailing his wife. I took a cab to the Hilton in Embassy Golf Links, checked in and freshened up.

Embassy Golf Links is one of the many software parks that fuel the economy of Bangalore city. Scores of engineers, migrants from all over the country are holed up in cubicles and benches tucked inside swanky buildings, busy in coding or attending to calls at odd hours.

An impressive office building near the front entrance houses IBM and Globosoft in two interconnected towers. I had enough filth on Selvam to give him the jitters, but not a theory on what had really happened. So, I decided to walk over to his office and see how he would react on being confronted.

I placed a spy pen in my breast pocket and wore a spy watch to record conversations. Then, I walked into the reception desk of Globosoft office and thumped a visiting card on the young girl sitting there. The visiting card mentioned me as Rajinder Singh, senior advocate of Bombay High Court. During my days in corporate espionage, I had created multiple fake identity cards and masqueraded as an advocate, a reporter, a doctor and a researcher at different times.

I demanded an audience with Anbu Selvam. The young girl asked me if I had an appointment.

"No, I don't," I said.

"You can't meet the MD without an appointment."

"Oh yes, I can. My client intends to file a sexual harassment suit against him and this is his last chance for a settlement. You better connect me to him or you would be sorry later you did not heed my advice now."

"Who was sexually harassed?" she asked curiously.

"Your rank is not commensurate to the question you ask, miss."

She asked me to take a seat, grabbed the visiting card and whispered something on an intercom phone. Within minutes a huge man, above six feet in height, with bushy hair and dark complexion came to me and introduced himself as Palani Kumar.

He started in a heavy Tamil accent, "MD is not in office. He has asked me to talk to you. I am the…"

"You are the head of security here," I interrupted. "I know. Swati told me about you."

I noticed the look of shock on his face and continued, "But I have been authorised to talk to Anbu Selvam only. If he is not here, I will give a number. Ask him to get in touch with me. I will tell him when and where to meet."

"You a lawyer?"

"Yes. I am a senior advocate in Bombay High Court and representative of Ms Swati Gupta Bhide in a legal matter that concerns Mr Anbu Selvam."

Palani smirked. "That's nat even her real name. Wait a minute. I have to talk to boss." Palani went away, furiously clicking into his smartphone and came back within a minute.

"Boss is in the office. Please come with me," he said. I followed him into an elevator while he pressed the call button for the fifth floor.

"So, where is Swati Gupta?" Palani asked as we entered the elevator. I chose to ignore the question, implying in a way that he is not important enough to know. His question did negate the possibility that the company had her locked up somewhere and orchestrated her vanishing.

Anbu Selvam had a markedly dark brown complexion and his big fat face was splattered with pimples. He was dressed in a white suit. Unlike Palani, he had a pretty neutral accent. He rose from his chair to shake my hand and I noticed that he was a small man, an inch or two taller than Bhide. His face was disproportionately larger than the rest of his body. There was another person in the room, a tall, muscular man in a tee and jeans, and lots of gold ornaments, whom he introduced as his brother Shashi Selvam.

"I must say Mr Singh, that I am intrigued by the nature of your business here. Swati's husband is an employee in our company and a good friend too. They had a fight and she has abruptly left him. The poor guy is running around searching for her. Where is she?" Anbu said.

"What I have to tell you is privileged. I need to speak with you in private," I said. I had a feeling that his brother and Palani did not know about his affair with Swati, a fact I wanted to use as leverage.

"I don't think that is necessary. Tamvi is a director in the company and Palani a senior executive."

"Even then, I insist. I am bound by codes of my legal practice." Palani and Shashi Selvam left the room before receiving any indication from Anbu Selvam.

"Ms Swati has hired me to handle a suit of sexual harassment against you. You misused your power as an employer to demand sexual favours from her. We have videos as well as evidence in the form of hotel log books in the period you forced her to tour Mumbai and sleep with you."

"Her case is not maintainable in court. She is an imposter and used fake certificates and a name to get employed in this office. She will be liable for criminal charges if she sues me."

"If she is an imposter, have you filed a case with the police?" I asked.

"No, for her husband's sake. He is a loyal employee and an old friend."

"An old friend whose wife you screw," I said sarcastically.

"She has definitely not been honest with you. Swati seduced me. She made repeated sexual overtures to me."

"Because you are short, dark and handsome, and she could not resist you? Or because you have swollen like a porker, and look as cute as one? A judge would not be convinced by your argument." I spoke like an insensitive prick so as to infuriate him. A man gives away a lot when infuriated. But he was utterly composed, rather assured of his looks.

"Bhide is shorter, fairer and cuter than me. A judge would not be convinced she married him."

"How do I know any of what you say is true?" I asked.

"I have evidence. WhatsApp messages in which she professes her love to me," Anbu said.

"Can I see?" I asked.

"Definitely. I will talk to my lawyer. We can meet you and Ms Swati as early as in the evening today. Is she in Bangalore?"

"No. She has recused herself from the settlement negotiations and has authorised me to handle all negotiations."

"She expects a settlement, eh?" he asked.

"Yes. Unless you want the videos to be out for public viewership."

"The girl is outrageous. She has the face to ask for a settlement!"

"Your wife, I am to believe, holds 60% of shares of your company. She is the owner of the company and you are almost an employee in the company. How do you think she would react to a scandal?" I spoke dramatically.

Selvam, surprisingly, was unaffected by my threat of defamation, and I found this disturbing.

"Where is Swati?" Selvam asked coldly.

"She has *explicitly* asked me not to reveal her location."

"What is her real name? Her PAN card and driving license copies submitted with our office are fake."

"It will be revealed at an appropriate time," I asserted.

"Then how do I know she has authorised you to represent herself?"

"I have her letter of authorization at my hotel. I can produce it in a formal meeting with your lawyer or you. I did not feel the need to bring it today since…"

Selvam interrupted, "By what name has she signed the authorisation? If she has signed as Swati Gupta, the authorisation is legally void."

Selvam had me cornered into an intellectual pit. I should have prepared my strategy before barging into his office. Selvam had outsmarted me – masquerading as an advocate – on a legal matter.

I was at a risk of blowing my cover, unless I could convince him that I am the dumbest senior advocate of a high court ever. I decided to make a quick exit.

"You have raised a valid question. I will consult my client and fix a time at which I can meet your lawyer. I guess I will have to reveal her real name at that point, as I exchange power of attorney with your advocate," I said and started to rise.

"Wait! You are not going anywhere without telling me where Swati is. Where is she?" Selvam said. I sensed threat and brazenness in his voice.

"I will have to consult my client to reveal that too. She has explicitly asked me not to reveal her location."

"How will you consult her? Over phone? You have her number, don't you?" Selvam said.

"Good day Mr Selvam," I said and hurried to the door. He pressed a calling bell and immediately his brother burst into the room with Palani.

"Don't tell me you people were eavesdropping on us like a couple of college girls," I said.

"Where is the bitch?" Anbu Selvam asked from behind me.

"Let me check my pockets," I said. "Oh wait. She isn't in here."

Shashi Selvam aimed a punch at my face, but I curved to my left and he missed me. I had sized him and Palani earlier. Palani, although massive in appearance, was just a mass of flesh, probably due to excessive intake of whey protein without any strength training. Shashi Selvam, on the other hand, was quick and deft. He boasted lean muscle mass on his arms and shoulders.

At six feet, I was taller than him. I had pumped good weight in my last few months of joblessness, more out of boredom than enthusiasm, and was confident of a strong mid-body and shoulders.

I drove a punch into Palani's skull and blocked a kick from Shashi Selvam with the other hand. In the time Palani took to react, I aimed for Selvam's abdomen, which I assessed as the weakest part of his body. He blocked my move with both hands and tried to pull me down. That was good for me; I aimed a kick directly between his legs.

Shashi Selvam yelped in pain. I shoved Palani to one side and opened the door, to find a heavy man standing just outside the door. He levered his hand up and hit me in the underside of my chin. I fell back with a thud. Palani jumped on me and deposited all his mass onto me. The other man entered the room and kicked me hard at my neck.

I was taken to an anteroom, an empty room with just an iron chair and a wooden table for furniture – evidently an interrogation room. I was made to sit in the iron chair in the middle of the room and my hands were tied behind my back with duct tape.

An interrogation room inside a cosmopolitan corporate office at the heart of a global software capital. I took some time to convalesce from the shock.

Meanwhile, half a dozen men surrounded my chair and volleyed punches at my face. Palani held my chair to stop it from toppling from the force of punches. I shot out expletives on their mothers and sisters, in response to which the blows stopped. Just when I was considering if I should be grateful to their mothers and sisters, Shashi Selvam came forward and drivelled his fist into my ribs. The pain was blinding.

Then Anbu Selvam said in his neutral, emotionless tone, "We don't want to harm Swati, if that's your concern. You tell us where the money is and we let you go. You don't, we will kill you."

Palani, who was standing behind the chair, frisked me and found my smartphone, but it was password protected. When he was unable to open it, I took another shot at threatening him.

"You aren't getting anything out of me this way. You have rubbed a high court senior advocate the wrong way. You let me go now and I will forget this ever happened. Else things may go ugly," I said, although none of them heeded to what I said.

They kept chewing furiously in Tamil. After a couple of minutes of more blabbering, deliberating and arguing, one of them, a short, skinny fellow, drew a pistol – a SIG Pro semi-automatic.

I was frightened. Seeing the turn of events, I understood that this was a caucus of serious lunatics, not white-collar types, and anyone among them could bump me off on slight indignation. I considered, for a moment, admitting to impersonation and begging for their forgiveness; however something about their attitude convinced me they would not buy it at this point.

The skinny fellow pointed the pistol at my chest and asked, "Where is Swati Gupta? Where is the money? Last chance!"

I was concerned that my murderers may not be avenged. I hadn't notified anyone about my visit to Globosoft office. Nor did I have a partner waiting for me outside the building. My wife, Bhide and Nidhi knew I was in Bangalore, but none of them would guess I barged into Globosoft office before vanishing.

As the skinny Tamil was pointing his semi-automatic at me, with a finger resting on the trigger, I shouted. "Okay! Okay!" I don't know about the money. I can only tell you what I know about Swati Gupta. She contacted me through email and claimed that Anbu Selvam was sexually assaulting her; that she has evidence by way of videography of his assaults. It raised my curiosity and I asked her to meet me in person. We met in a crowded mall in Mumbai. She handed me some videos and gave details of how Selvam used to harass her. When I asked her about whereabouts, she said she was in hiding because Selvam here knows she has the videos and that there are goons hunting for her, apparently sent by Selvam. She filled me in about the case on a *need to know* basis. It worked all right for me since I was still in the discovery process. She gave me the impression that we could make money by settling the evidence with Selvam."

I spoke at a fast pace, so as to give the impression that I was confessing the truth.

"Hou do you get in touch with her then?" Shashi Selvam said.

"She has given me a number. I have to phone her from my number only, for her to respond."

"How do we know you are not lying?" he asked.

"Try sending a message to her number from my mobile."

"What is the phone's password?"

"It has a fingerprint password."

"The display is asking for a passcode."

"Yes it does, but there is no passcode. The homepage appears as soon as my fingerprint is scanned. Let me show you her number."

I hoped none of them was a smartphone enthusiast. My phone was a Samsung Galaxy E5, which, anyone following smartphones knows, does not have fingerprint access features.

Anbu Selvam nodded at Palani who was standing behind me. Palani removed the duct tapes binding my hands and showed me my smartphone. I was feeling dizzy from all the punches I took, yet appreciated the small window of opportunity I was handed. I held my smartphone in my left hand and feigned pressing my thumb at its surface. The skinny fellow's attention was on my phone screen.

I jumped on him, gave a blow on his neck, and pulled his pistol. As he reeled from the pain, the semi-automatic easily slipped into my hand. I drove my elbow into his chest, and he fell.

They were least expecting this, having concluded that I was sufficiently mauled to be able to show any agility. I hit a large ogre standing to my right with the butt of the pistol. A space opened for me as he fell. I jumped and got away from the circle, then pointed the pistol at the circle and moved deftly to the door. I went out, that is, into Anbu Selvam's cabin, and bolted the interrogation room from outside.

I scoured through desk drawers in Anbu Selvam's cabin as they tried to break open the door, collected whatever files and diaries I could lay my hands on, and dashed out. I bolted Anbu Selvam's cabin from outside on my way out. The receptionist looked at me with an expression of incredulity as I was exiting.

"Tell your MD I am coming back. I am gonna screw him and everyone else involved in this," I told her pointing at my bloody face. "And you!"

5

Mucky Secrets

The Hilton in Golf Links was three blocks away from Globosoft office. I hurried across to the hotel, although I was aware that the tech-park's campus security had me immune from any attack in the open.

Once at the hotel, I asked the receptionist for a duplicate key-card to my room. She looked at my grisly face and blood-stained shirt with suppressed anxiety and asked if I was okay.

I shrugged and broadly smiled at her. "Never felt better," I said. She revulsed, probably on seeing more blood on my gums.

She offered to send an ice pack and a first aid box to my room, to which I responded with a broader smile and an unfeigned thank you.

Back in the room, I rummaged the mini-bar for alcohol. I emptied two mini-packs of Chivas Regal to numb the pain and ordered for more from room service. I took good time to dress my wounds and clean up. I was badly hurt and needed a trip to the hospital, maybe a few stitches too. But first, I needed someone to watch my back.

Barging into Globosoft office was lousy of me. And having no back-up was lousier. In the business of detection, people get killed for lousy mistakes and I had committed a blunder.

Resolving to better myself at this job, I opened my laptop and looked for Nidhi's number in the phone book. I had lost my only phone in the squabble to get out of Anbu Selvam's clutches. I phoned Nidhi from the hotel landline and pleaded with her to rush to the Hilton. I also asked her to get a spare phone and a SIM card on the way.

Although I could not understand any of the blabber of Anbu Selvam and his gang in Tamil, I had all that conversation recorded in my spy-pen. I connected the spy-pen to the USB drive of my laptop and extracted an audio file. I phoned Parthivan, an old acquaintance and a Tamil, and asked him if he could listen to the audio file and translate it for me. He agreed and I emailed the audio file to him.

I dialled my telecom service provider and got my number's SIM card blocked. I also wanted to report a theft of my mobile phone, but that could wait. I phoned Bhide and asked him for more info on his boss.

"He is a good man. He respects hard work," Bhide said.

"No, Bhide. He is a businessman. What kind of a businessman is he? Is he a shrewd businessman? Is he an opportunist or an innovator? How does he deal with his business associates? I want answers to these questions."

"He is a hardworking businessman. I can introduce you to him. He is very busy, but he will meet anyone I take to him," Bhide said.

"My great fortune!" I said sarcastically, although I was quite sure Bhide could not catch my sarcasm. "What do your colleagues at work gossip about him? Or are they all awed by him?"

"No, they are not pleased. They believe he exploits us and pays below the market standards."

"There is a charitable trust called Malabar Children Education Trust. What does it do?"

"It donated funds for children's education till a few years back. I do not know the specifics, but I handle the accounts. It used to donate money to some orphanages and schools in western Karnataka and Kerala"

"Any name you can recall?"

"Difficult to recall. Let me see some madrasas providing free education to minorities in Mangalore and Kasaragod areas on Malabar coast… then some coffee plantations in Coorg and Chikmagalur for education of workers' children. I don't remember specifics, and since my transfer to Chennai office, I have lost access to its accounts."

"The trust got its money from abroad. Where did it get money from?"

"Cannot say that! Money usually came from bank accounts in Dubai. Roopalaxmi madam is known for her charity works."

"Why did the donation dry out so suddenly?"

"I don't know. Why is that important?" Bhide asked, surprised at this sudden interrogation session.

"Never mind. You had given me your wife's phone number. Did she maintain any other number?"

"No!"

"Can you get me the phone numbers of Anbu Selvam, Shashi Selvam, Roopalaxmi Sivanarayanan, Palani, and all people who work for Palani?"

"I will text their numbers to you. I don't know the people who work for Palani, but I can find from him."

"No, you need to get their numbers discreetly. Don't tell them that you have employed a private eye to investigate your wife's disappearance. Don't tell them anyone asked for their numbers," I explained. "We have to be clear on this. Do you understand?"

"Ok… yes," he replied.

"Now, send their numbers to Nidhi's phone. I have lost my phone," I informed and hung up.

▼

Four pegs of scotch arrived in my room with fried fish and a bucket of finger chips. I undraped the window screens and sat down by the window with the papers I had picked from Selvam's chamber.

I flipped through the papers as I took gulps of scotch. Some of the scribblings were useless, such as reminders and notes on meetings with vendors. However, the diary contained details of bank accounts in Cyprus, Dubai, Mauritius, and a host of other tax havens – even Saint Kitts and Nevis. A bunch of companies incorporated in British Virgin Islands (BVI) were listed in one page with dates and figures against them. Details of a trust registered in Jersey along with a bank account number, user id and password for online access, were neatly written on one page.

There was a lot of unnecessary information in the diary that I could use as leverage, but I did not see anything of much substance for the case. Parking money in tax havens has become the new normal in these times.

Tax havens are used by multinational corporations to reduce their tax liability in host countries. There is no surprise in it, as the practice has become quite rampant. Globosoft, being a contractor for foreign firms, would naturally be tempted to park a part of its income in tax havens to escape paying tax in India.

On reaching the end of the diary, I observed a list of names and figures against them on the inside of the back cover. Handwriting was the same as on the other pages – which I surmised was Anbu Selvam's.

Not familiar with the names, I googled them. To my surprise, most of them were Imams from madrasas across south India. Two active political leaders from minority communities in Kerala also found mention in the list. Few names were generic and did not match any specific personality upon googling. I was profiling the names when Parthivan called.

"Hey Digyen, I heard the recording you sent me. The people in the recording are beating up someone, while that guy is screaming and shouting and swearing and crying. He appeared to be you. So?" Parthivan said.

"Yeah, that's me. I was doing the swearing and shouting – but no crying. What are they talking about?" I asked, trying to keep the conversation focussed.

"Well, they are talking about some money and are debating if you know about it. Some girl has taken the money and they are desperate to get it back. One person – someone with a neutral accent – says that the girl will not send someone to extort more money after what she has done. So you are an imposter. A second person – one with a strong accent – says Kedia may have sent you. Others do not have a high opinion of Kedia and think he might have conned them.

"Then another guy says that they cannot rule out the possibility that you are part of the racket the girl is running. They expect you to give up and confess, but you don't seem to be confessing. One guy proposes to shoot you in your leg to make you confess. His name is probably Bala, and he comes out as intent to shoot you."

"That bastard was pointing a semi-automatic at me," I said, tensely recalling how I faced off with the barrel of the pistol just a couple of hours back.

"Look, at times the voices are not clear because they are all talking at the same time," Parthivan continued. "On top of that, you are shouting. The second person does not like the idea of shooting you and says they must consult someone called Lokka before harming you. The first person says he can take the decision and Lokka should not be bothered with such small issues, but the second person chides him.

"Then a third person blames the first person for the mess. He says that had he kept his dick in his pants and not been a *pundai nakki* – it's a swear word – this would not have happened. He says they should call Lokka before deciding on any course of action. Then Bala says there is no harm in intimidating you. He then threatens you in English. That's the gist of it."

"The person with the neutral accent is Anbu Selvam. He is their boss. Anything else you could pick from his chatter?"

Parthivan paused for a moment and said, "I don't think he is the boss. See, another person called him a *pundai nakki*, which is a harsh swear word and one does not abuse even a former boss with such words. These people are all informal with each other and at the same rank. They use swear words like *ommalla okka* and *sunniya umbu* that you won't use in civil gatherings. These people are pure rowdies. How did you come across such persons?"

"Actually they are the senior management of a software company in Bangalore. And their clients are hi-fi tech companies in America and Europe."

"Seriously? Their accent was unusual. Except the guy with a neutral accent, the rest are from a rural area. Their accents are similar, so is their dialect. I can't place their dialect, but it's not the Tamil that people of class speak."

"The person with the neutral accent and another one of the guys – perhaps the one who swears at him – are brothers."

I thanked Parthivan and disconnected. Then I downed the remaining scotch while waiting for Nidhi. The bruises still pained. So I ordered more and drank more.

The Selvams and the revenge I fancied on them recurred in my thoughts time and again.

▼

I woke up to find Nidhi doting over me. She pouted and made a funny face that a mother makes when her baby wakes up. She was looking stunning, as ever. Her silky hair, fine eyelashes and supple cheek reeked of hours in the parlour. She had come in a sky-blue shirt and dark blue parallels, and emanated a heavy smell of jasmine-scented perfume.

"How long have you been here?" I asked.

"About an hour."

"You could have woken me up"

"You were sleeping! You did not respond to the dozen odd calls from the reception. I told them down there that you are my husband and I need a duplicate key – created a ruckus when they did not give me the key. Finally, the manager escorted me in. I got into your room some ten minutes back."

I rose and hugged her warmly. Nidhi has been many things to me, but a good friend above all else.

"What happened? Were you mobbed?" Nidhi asked.

I poured water from a flask into a glass and gulped it. Painful irritation from the wounds was back.

"Swati Gupta has conned Bhide and his employers. Swati – or whatever her real name is – used Bhide as bait to reach his boss. She fished Bhide out from the social network, tried to seduce him but realised that he is an idiot. Then, she probably tried to fish for other employees of Globosoft, but probably could not find anyone with an approach to the MD, Anbu Selvam.

"Most employees in Globosoft are engineers working on outsourced projects. They would not have easy access to the MD. Bhide had unbridled access to him, as he reported to Selvam. So, she was back to using Bhide as bait. She told an incredulous story about being the illegitimate daughter of a Bengali political leader, which Bhide eagerly bought. She married him, reached the MD, and started screwing him. The MD himself is a man with low self-esteem—"

"How do you know she was screwing the MD?" she interrupted.

"I checked with the hotel the MD stays in, when in Mumbai. She used to stay with him in the same room. The MD Anbu Selvam introduced her to the hotel manager as his wife."

"Are you sure?" she looked at me incredulously.

"I am not sure if they were fucking or not. She lied to Bhide that she was staying in some other hotel. But she was staying with Anbu Selvam. Same hotel, same room. Anbu Selvam and Bhide's wife. These are the facts.

"Now, one fine day she manages to rob the company of a substantial stash of cash and flees. The company's goons investigate and realise that her identity is fake. They do tell Bhide that she is a fraud, but do not give him any details. The cash is probably black money, due to which they are behaving so secretively. So Bhide believes she has been kidnapped by the Bengali politician."

"Poor Bhide," Nidhi whispered, more to herself. I offered her a glass of water. She took it and sipped on it.

"What happened to you?"

"I went into Globosoft office, some three blocks from this hotel and made some enquiries. Globosoft – apparently a software company – has goons in its payrolls. There is an interrogation room in its office, adjacent to the MD's chamber. They took me in there and tortured me. I am lucky I escaped from there."

"Have you reported to the police?" she asked, looking concerned.

"No. Bhide had approached the police to lodge an FIR. They did not entertain his request. Selvam has some influence on the local police too. It's no use approaching the authorities without clear evidence. They will sabotage the investigation."

"Oh god! I knew the company was up to some mischief when Bhide told me the company did not allow him to lodge an FIR."

"It is full of muck, Nidhi. Its security team includes the criminal types who do not hesitate to kill. The company develops software for foreign clients. It has no local customer; yet it pays politicians and, oddly, Muslim clerics. I have found a diary from the MD's chamber that has accounts of payments made to such persons. Usually politicians are funded by those who have regular business with the government – such as contractors and builders, who need political support for multiple clearances and approvals.

"Globosoft needs no such approvals – not even from the pollution control authorities. It does not do any land acquisition. It has taken its office space on lease from the tech-park owner. It has no reason to pay kickbacks. But it still does. This raises another question, how does it generate so much cash to pay kickbacks?

"We know beyond doubt that the company handles a large volume of cash. The imposter we know as Swati Gupta had some insider information about it. She reached Selvam's bed and from there to the cash. She has run away with a good amount, given the desperation Selvam's gang is showing to find her."

Nidhi frowned and went for the minibar. At times, long before Sneha came into my life, I had fondled and kissed her. There were no strings attached, and she was clear there won't be any strings attached if we made love. Still, we never got around to that. Not making love with Nidhi when I could remains a pent up regret in me.

She came back with a diet coke and sat across me on the bed. I stared at her apple cheek and large eyes.

"What now?" she asked.

"You tell me, what now?" I was puzzled.

"We still have to find this woman."

"Why? Anbu Selvam must have appointed the best of detectives to find her. His own in-house security team appears to be quite capable," I said.

"Bhide will insist that we find her. He is madly in love with her."

"Why should he waste money? What will he do once he finds her?"

"There are many equations working here, Digyen. That woman is his wife. He is in love with her. He can't think about it as objectively as you can. I will try to reason with him, but I think he will insist on us finding her," she said confidently.

"Okay. The case intrigues me. I will keep digging."

"What do you plan on doing?"

"Bhide must have sent you some phone numbers. I will get their CDRs for the last few months. I will try to find out—"

"What is CDR?" she interrupted to ask.

"Call Detail Record. It's a report generated by the telecom service provider that gives details of calls made and calls received. I will extract the CDR of Selvam, his associates, and Swati Gupta. That's a starting point."

"I did not know you could get such a report," Nidhi said.

"It's illegal to get CDRs. Accessing such data violates the user's privacy. That is why service providers can share CDRs only with specific law enforcement agencies. But then, it's the best way to cover ground in an investigation. I am using a source to get their CDRs. I am sure the detectives employed by Selvam must have already extracted Swati Gupta's CDR by now. If he has employed the police to find her, they can anyway extract CDR."

6

Party Scenes

It was six in the evening by the time I got my wounds treated and came out of the hospital. Luckily, no wound was severe enough to require stitches. My face was nevertheless swollen and the doctor had recommended a few days' rest.

I have been on rest since my last employment and was in no mood for more; especially now, when I was restless to grab Selvam by his balls and make him scream.

The next person on my itinerary was Sanjay Mallya. An old acquaintance from my days in corporate employment, he moves around in elite circles in Bangalore. He has deep connections in the megalithic state bureaucracy and local police, and cosies up with local leaders of all hue and agenda. I decided he would be the best person to source local gossip and local contacts.

Mallya was in town and was hosting a party later in the evening. He called me over to the Tao Terraces pub later in the evening. Nidhi wanted to accompany me, but I insisted I had to meet my source alone.

I had already phoned Saby Biswas and appraised him of the case on my way to the hospital. He appeared disturbed on hearing that I was beaten up and readily agreed to get the CDRs from his sources.

I sent him eight phone numbers – of Swati, Anbu Selvam, his wife and brother, Palani, and three persons reporting to Palani – and he promised to get back.

Biswas da's phone came as I was reaching the Hilton.

"Da, any update?"

"Yes. I have got your CDRs. I am sending them to your email. Make good use of them. It's becoming increasingly difficult to lay hands on these reports."

"Thanks da."

"You are welcome. Now Digyen, I cursorily went through some CDRs and found that this Roopalaxmi lady is a high flyer. She does not stay in India much, but the few days she stays in India, she converses regularly with biggies in Delhi – socialites, top reporters, ambassadors and some lawmakers too. Anbu Selvam is in constant touch with a cop and had phoned him today too multiple times – one phone call was of some thousand seconds duration, possibly after your escape from his office. Truecaller throws up the name 'ACP Bopanna'."

"Makes sense. I will profile this cop too."

"Keep a back-up Digyen, someone with a gun license."

"Am on it, da."

▼

I reached the Tao Terraces an hour before midnight. It was a rooftop pub, that had had an energetic and youthful crowd, with a large number of expats.

It took me some time to trace Mallya in the wilderness of smartly dressed young girls and thick smoke. Mallya is a skinny guy in his late forties, but always dresses in youthful attire. This evening he was dressed in a black sleeveless top and jeans. He was smoking a joint while two blonde European girls flanked him on either side. One was in a sari draped with care to expose her bosoms and back through a backless blouse. The other was in black, single piece latex. He spread his hands out on seeing me, and warmly embraced me.

"How you bro! Long time," Mallya said. "You have forgotten your dear friend."

But before I could say anything, he introduced me to the girls flanking him, "Meet my friend Digyen Burmah. Real stud!"

He pulled up a waiter and asked him to get me a drink. I ordered a whisky sour with eggs. He was sitting in a group and introduced me to others partying with him. The party was in honour of some official from the local pollution control board.

The official, a bespectacled man with a paunch and a boring demeanour, looked out of place. Dressed in a striped formal shirt and trousers, it seemed he had landed at the party directly from his office. Nevertheless, Mallya made sure that he was comfortable. Two Russian ladies had been put to the job. They were making some small talk and keeping him busy. The official was accompanied by a friend, who was in a hurry to gulp down the free liquor. Both were hungrily, but shyly, eyeing the Russian chicks.

A teenager sporting a neatly pruned beard, the kind that became popular when Virat Kohli sported it, was the other male member of Mallya's party. He was more of an assistant, placing orders and serving drinks and food.

Music was loud and Mallya was already oscillating. Few other girls joined us. I realised it would be pointless discussing anything with him before the party got over. So I enjoyed my drink and did small talk with a Bengali girl who worked as a dentist in the city and was a regular in Mallya's parties.

I was out of place with the merry making crowd, as my thoughts were fixated on the case. Yet, I was determined not to be perceived as a bore; so I acquiesced when the Bengali girl asked me for a dance.

Few of her friends joined us after sometime. Mallya also monkeyed in, followed by the sari-clad blonde. Then Mallya cajoled the visibly reluctant bureaucrat from the pollution control board to join the dance.

The clerk, somewhat high by now, cupped his palms into cobra hoods and brought them together over his forehead. Then he did a *naagin* dance, the weird cobra-like gyrating that is popular in marriage processions these days.

His naagin dance became an instant hit among the girls, and the blonde in sari tried to copy his moves. Everyone, it appears, was programmed to humour the important man.

I saw an opportunity and slipped back to my chair. I peered over the crowd towards the DJ, to find the reason for the sudden change of theme from EDM to the naagin dance.

Mallya was standing there with the DJ and waving in my direction. The bureaucrat got his cue and excitedly fell on the floor on his back. Maintaining the posture of cupped palms over his forehead, he swirled and rotated on the floor. All members of Mallya's party, which had swelled by now to about a dozen girls and half a dozen guys, surrounded him and clapped.

Later, Mallya asked me to go with him to an after-party. He was accompanied by the blonde girl.

"Can't come, bhai. Had a long day. Will catch up tomorrow. I am here for a few more days," I shouted into his ear.

"But you can't miss the after-party bro. The best party animal in town has organised it."

"No bhai, another time. Look at my face, how miserable I look. I need to rest and tend to this swollen cheek," I reasoned.

"Okay. But you have to come to the after-party. It's going to be mind blowing. Real action in Bangalore is at an after-party," Mallya said and the blonde nodded knowingly.

"I see that Bong girl taking a liking for you. She will be all lonely in the after-party if you don't turn up," Mallya said, and the blonde appeared concerned.

"Have to call my wife also. She is all alone in Mumbai and has not been keeping well of late," I lied. Mallya was insistent. Finally, we decided that I would accompany Mallya to a condo where the after-party would take place, and leave after a drink. The clerk was duly escorted and established in a vehicle with attendant ladies. Others in Mallya's party separated themselves into groups and decided to meet up at the after-party.

Mallya was driving an Audi Q7 and asked me to accompany him. His demeanour changed immediately after taking the wheel. While he appeared stoned and tipsy in the party, he talked like a sober businessman once inside the car.

"Tell me yaar, what brings you to Bangalore?"

"I have taken up freelance work. Just helping an old friend with a personal issue. How is business here?"

"Business is good. There is good money in Bangalore. Just yesterday I fixed a deal in which a private equity (PE) fund has agreed to invest twenty million dollars into an e-learning start-up. I am getting two percent."

"Two percent?" I whistled. "Start-ups are giving that much for securing funding?"

"Some do. Two percent is nothing. The PE fund managers are getting five percent back. The money will go from the start-up to private firms owned by relatives of the fund managers.

"That pollution control board official you met today was creating problems in another deal – a wind power plant project worth three hundred crores in coastal Karnataka. Eight percent of the capex is on liaisoning. I made the land acquisition, got right-of-way from farmers, approvals from panchayat, ministry, everything. Minus expenses, my take home is one percent.

"This official is new. No one in my network has a rapport with him. His boss is an upright officer and is ready to give environmental clearance on merits. But this guy was playing delaying tactics. So I decided I will take the bull by its horns," Mallya jeered and said. "Someone will blow him today, and I will make sure someone blows him every day till he gives his clearance."

"Nice. A former associate had phoned me a few days back asking for a contact. He is working for a Brazilian MNC that wants to open a heavy electrical equipment factory in Bangalore. It is not getting land lease from the state industrial development board here – Karnataka Industrial Areas Development Board (KIADB), although the board has a clear policy. He was looking for a consultant to sort out the matter," I said.

Mallya does not do any free favour, so I had to dangle a bone for him.

"If you have any contact in KIADB, you can take up the work. They will pay well," I said.

"Yes, yes. I have friends in KIADB. I can highlight their grievance at the right place," Mallya said.

I slowly veered the topic to the help I needed.

"Do you know one Assistant Commissioner of Police (ACP) Bopanna?" I asked.

"ACP South-East zone? He is a thorough bastard. Both he and his DCP are," Mallya said.

"Why?"

"He does not behave like an officer. He is basically a middleman. Recently he kidnapped an industrialist I know. The industrialist had taken a cash loan from a Gujarati moneylender. He defaulted on some interest payments because of liquidity issues. Bopanna kidnapped this industrialist and kept him in a police mess. He asked the guy's wife to pay the moneylender entire principal with interest and a baseless default penalty to release him. I helped her sell a property to pay up. The property could have fetched more, but because she sold it in distress, she took whatever the buyer offered."

I was sure Mallya would have taken his cut for helping the wife sell her property, and Bopanna would have taken his cut from the moneylender.

"I may displease Bopanna when helping my friend in his case. How wise is it to have a face-off with him?" I asked.

"Don't worry about him. He worked fine under the patronage of the former commissioner. The present Commissioner of Police is looking for an opportunity to throw him out of field postings. The Director General also disapproves of him. If you have a genuine complaint against him, I can arrange for an audience with the commissioner and DG."

"I will tell you if the need arises. By the way, I need to hire a bodyguard."

Mallya looked at me inquisitively. "What do *you* need a bodyguard for?"

"Not exactly a bodyguard. An assistant. Someone to watch my back. Someone who knows the local language and can tackle a rowdy if I come across one."

"This is my city. Call me if anyone bothers you. But if you insist, I will look for a guy for you. How much will you pay?"

"Pay will not be a problem, but I will need him only for a month."

"I think I already have a person in mind. Let me talk to him tomorrow and get back to you."

Then, I showed a list of names to Mallya and asked him if he found anything common among them. The list contained the names I had found in Anbu Selvam's diary. Mallya knew many of them personally.

"This guy is a complete fraud," he said pointing a finger at a name. "Poses as a leader of minority groups in Bangalore, but exploits them to meet his own ends. He has a strong following among poor Muslims of Uttara Kannada area. He uses his mass appeal to control local politicians and local administration, even while running a drug racket in Mangalore area."

"This one was raided by the income tax department during recent elections," he continued, pointing at another name. "A lot of cash was found from his possession."

"Local elections, you mean?"

"Assembly elections."

"I presume all these men in the list were active in elections," I said.

"Yes! This guy himself contested from somewhere near Bellari, while these two clerics supported independent candidates in Mangalore," Mallya said pointing to few names.

"How much cash is involved in these elections?"

"Some six crores per candidate per assembly constituency – on an average. And that is in Karnataka. In Tamil Nadu, it's higher, at eight to ten crores"

"That's filthy high! Does every candidate spend that much?"

"It's a complex game. Some candidates are honest – if they get elected, it's because of their mass following. On the other side of the spectrum are industrial belts, where candidates can spend as high as twenty crores. These candidates spend money to patronise rowdy elements, who help the candidates in creating problems for business owners.

"Business owners donate to the candidate to protect them from the rowdies. Here, the candidate runs a protection racket. Even if the candidate does not win, he gains loyalty of rowdies, which he encashes in future endeavours.

"And if the candidate wins, he may get returns twenty times over. This is how the cost-benefit equation works in southern states."

"Do software and BPO companies also pay protection money?" I asked.

"No. They are footloose, and can shift out of the state anytime. That's why they are given special VIP treatment. Their customers are usually in America. They also do not need any approval from local authorities. So why will they pay?"

"Got you!" I said. The picture was slowly getting clearer.

7

The Hawala Agent

I reached my room late in the night and had a fitful sleep. I woke up when the hotel reception called and informed me that one Puwaiya had an appointment with me.

I informed them that I had never heard that name and went back to sleep. But, the receptionist phoned back and told me that he had come on Sanjay Mallya's reference. I grudgingly asked her to send him upstairs.

I was in shorts when Puwaiya entered my room. The man was dressed in a dirty shirt and trousers. He was a frail man who could not hold himself steady. He swayed the entire time he was standing in my room. His arms were literally hanging over hunched shoulders. He looked tired and wizened. I wondered if he could aim a gun at a target.

"Do you have a gun license?" I asked, to keep the conversation going.

"Yes," Puwaiya said, and pulled out a .357 Magnum from under his shirt. He was still oscillating. The revolver's weight probably overwhelmed him, for his arm also shivered. With multiple forces working on keeping the revolver unsteady, his aim was too random to be predicted. I wondered which part of the room I should dive to take cover, in case he accidentally pulls the trigger.

"I meant a gun license, not the gun."

"Oh! Yes license," Puwaiya said and took out a paper from his trouser pocket. It was a photocopy of a license to carry a .357 Magnum.

"Have you worked as a bodyguard or gunman anywhere? Maybe for a bank or private security company?" I prodded.

"Sir, I working with Mutthapa Rai. Now get pension from Anna. So no work," Powaiya replied.

"Who Mutthapa Rai?" I asked. Puwaiya smiled shyly and shrugged. I contacted Mallya, but he did not pick up. I cannot expect him to be awake this early after attending the after party.

"Why does he give you a pension?" I figured it would be rude to reject him directly, since he had come with Mallya's recommendation.

"I took revenge on Anna's enemies. Anna gave me flat and pension. I am Anna's number one gunslinger"

"When did Mallya call you to meet me?"

"Night. Yesterday night."

By now, I could smell the stench of cheap liquor on Puwaiya's breath. Great! It was ten in the morning, and he was already drunk. Who comes to a job interview all drunk?

"Will this Mutthapa Rai give you a recommendation? Why don't you give me his number?" I asked. I was looking for reasons to defer recruiting him.

"Anna is a big man. Anna may not meet you sir. I will take you to meet Anna when you want."

Oh, is it? Puwaiya's deference piqued my interest. I googled for Mutthapa Rai on my smartphone, only to find that he was the biggest gangster of Bangalore. His Wikipedia page said that he used to have links with Dawood Ibrahim at some time. He was deported from UAE in 2002, after which he was grilled by the CBI, IB, RAW and Karnataka Police. Due to lack of substantial evidence, he was later acquitted. Now he was a social activist and a philanthropist.

I was impressed. If this drunk idiot really worked with an underworld don, he fit the bill. I asked him about his pay expectations. He demanded twelve thousand rupees for a month, same as my room's tariff for two nights. I offered him twenty thousand rupees, and sealed the deal.

I wondered how my wife would describe it. *The cocky pseudo-detective meets his match in a drunken loafer.*

I sent Puwaiya downstairs with instructions to be at my beck and call daily between ten in the morning and eight in the evening, and started analysing the CDRs Biswas da had sent me.

I stayed in my hotel room for four days, in which I tended to my wounds and analysed the voluminous data from the CDRs of Swati Gupta, Selvam, and his cronies. The CDRs provided data of all phone calls made or received by these phone users for a three-month period that ended a week after Swati Gupta's disappearance.

Swati Gupta's phone was registered in her name. She might have submitted forged documents to get the phone. She regularly called Anbu Selvam, Bhide, Palani and two phone numbers in Nepal. She called Nepal in the evening daily, almost religiously, and spoke for hours. You don't talk business for hours daily; this must be a friend or family. She had frequent messaging conversations with Anbu Selvam and Palani, often in late nights as well.

The frequent messaging with Palani was unusual. Palani was head of security, and ideally should not have much professional dealing with the MD's personal staff. *Was Palani also screwing her? Or was the entire office screwing her?*

A day before she disappeared, Swati had called Nepal from the Nariman Point area of Mumbai, and talked for almost half an hour. This is where Hotel Royale is located. She might have called her friend in Nepal from the hotel. She made frequent calls to Palani that day, all calls landing from a telecom tower located in Nariman Point.

She made an early morning call to a second number in Nepal, on the day she disappeared. Then, there was a short call from Bhide, probably to wish her a good morning. From there, she probably moved to Kalbadevi. Her tower location was in Kalbadevi when Palani phoned her at 11:15 a.m., 11:46 a.m., and 12:15 p.m. She phoned Palani at 01:11 p.m. when she was somewhere near Parel. She got a call from an unknown number in another ten minutes, when she was near Dadar. She got another call from the same unknown number twenty minutes later, when she was near Vakola Police Station.

Swati again called this unknown caller at 1:46 p.m., when she was near Santacruz airport. She was in Borivali at 2:59 p.m., when she got a call from Palani. This was the last call on her number. Her phone went dead after this point.

It appeared that Swati went to Kalbadevi from Hotel Royale in the morning, and went directly from there to the international airport. The shortest route from Kalbadevi to the airport in Santacruz goes through Parel, Dadar and Vakola. At the airport, curiously, she does not take a flight. She goes from there to Borivali.

Palani was in Bangalore on the day Swati disappeared. His phone showed calls to many persons in Karnataka and Tamil Nadu over the period the CDR covered. Although he had behaved like a sociopath with me, apparently he was a well-networked person. Through Truecaller, I could identify that some phone numbers he spoke with belonged to politicians and clerics in Selvam's diary.

I scourged Anbu Selvam's phone for international calls. To maintain all those offshore accounts mentioned in his diary, he must be making frequent calls to bankers overseas. But his CDR did not show any overseas calls. His foreign visits were also infrequent.

But I did manage to identify Kedia, who Selvam and his cronies were referring to in their conversation. His name is Ramkrishna Kedia. His Facebook profile showed that he is a financial advisor and operates from an office in Kalbadevi.

The CDRs revealed an important clue, that all was not well in Selvam's marriage. He had short and infrequent conversations with his wife. His wife stayed overseas most of the time and spent her days in India in Delhi. Selvam, his brother Shashi, Palani and other cronies working for Palani flew to Delhi whenever she came to India. But it appeared that Selvam did not spend much time with Roopalaxmi. Tower location data showed that they slept at different places.

As Biswas da had pointed out, Roopalaxmi knew the who's who of Indian polity.

I got the CDR of Swati's unknown caller and Kedia from Biswas da. Apparently, the unknown caller's number was unregistered. It was issued by Tata Docomo on the same day and was used to call Swati only. Tata Docomo disconnected the phone in a day because the subscriber had not given his KYC details.

The unknown caller was at Delhi airport at ten in the morning, when he made a call to Docomo's customer care centre. He was in Mumbai's Santacruz airport when he first called Swati at 1:21 p.m. Definitely, Swati had gone to the airport to meet him. She went to Borivali after meeting him.

Kedia's CDR showed that he stuck to a fixed routine. His house was somewhere in the Lower Parel area, from where he started daily between 9 and 9:30 a.m., and reached his office by 9:45 a.m. His office was located in Kalbadevi, where he stayed till after 7 p.m., and then left for his house. His CDR showed high volume of conversations with people in India as well as with people in Dubai, Singapore and Hong Kong. He received or made at least two hundred calls daily.

What kind of financial advisor broods over a mobile phone all day long, instead of bank statements and mutual fund forms? All clues lead me to one conclusion. Kedia is a Hawala agent.

I called Sunil Jain, a Hawala agent who maintains a small, dingy, pawn shop in Kalbadevi and enquired about his business.

"So Sunil ji," I said after exchanging initial pleasantries, "I need to move two boxes to Dubai. How many days will you take?" Box is a code word Hawala dealers of Mumbai prefer for a crore of rupees.

"Two days, Burmah bhai. It can be moved on the same day if it's urgent, but will cost extra."

"What's the rate these days?"

"Three paisa on a rupee. Best price in Kalbadevi, Burmah bhai."

"I have an offer for two paisa."

"No one manages at that low commission these days. I am offering the best price because of our old relation."

"Kedia is ready to transfer at two percent," I said.

"Who? Which Kedia?"

"Ramakrishna Kedia. His shop is in your neighbourhood."

"Oh, Kediaji! How can you compare him with us? Jain family of Johari Bazaar has been in this business for six generations now. Such is our reputation that we get walk-in customers everyday. People blindly trust us with their paisa."

I interrupted his self-marketing by asking, "Kedia is not trustworthy?"

"I did not say that. See, Kedia ji handles big volumes, so offers lower rates at times. Sometimes he cannot manage his volumes and takes support from others. I have helped him many times. You must have reached him with some references, no? He is an upstart – a Marwari from Calcutta without any background in our business. Can you trust him with two boxes, just on the basis of references?"

This was enough input for me, for now. Ramkrishna Kedia is a Hawala agent. Either Selvam was sending cash abroad through him, or bringing in cash from overseas. Swati Gupta took off with the money.

I could now appreciate why Selvam and his cronies were suspicious of Kedia. Cash transactions happen in closed networks. Outsiders cannot be aware of these transactions. Someone on the inside was helping Swati Gupta.

One last clue I needed to pursue from the CDR data analysis was the person in Nepal Swati Gupta was speaking with. She spoke with this person daily, for long hours. This person was the best bet to reach Swati.

I reached out to a friend in the foreign services for a contact in Nepal. This friend connected me with his colleague in India's embassy in Kathmandu, who connected me with Bidhya Chhetri, an investigative journalist working freelance in Nepal. I was assured that Bidhya is resourceful and has handled profile verifications for the embassy on a freelance basis.

I spoke with Bidhya and appraised her about the case without going into the specifics. Bidhya studied in Kathmandu and Delhi, and had been working as a journalist for two decades. I also found her fee very reasonable, given that her husband works in the Metropolitan Police department of Kathmandu.

I sent her a formal offer by email along with the two phone numbers in Nepal whom Swati spoke with. Bidhya needed a day's time to get the caller's identity, and a fortnight to conduct comprehensive field verification.

True to her commitment, she got back to me in a day with the two phone numbers. Both were mobile phones; one was registered in the name of Ms Preeti Gurung, and the other in the name of Arjun Gurung.

Bidhya also sent me a scanned copy of their applications to the telecom service provider NCell. The application of Preeti Gurung contained a declaration of her address in Kathmandu city, and a passport size photograph.

It was Swati Gupta's photograph on the application. Preeti Gurung is Swati Gupta.

8

Striking the Deal

I got a call from the hotel reception on Wednesday morning, informing me that ACP Bopanna had come to investigate a matter. Having locked myself in a room with a laptop for days together, I had forgotten the sense of time. It was about noon, but I had not had a bath.

ACP Bopanna wanted to come up to my room. I gave clear instruction to the receptionist to make him wait in the lobby till I came down. I was in no hurry. I brushed, had a shower and changed into a fresh polo shirt and jeans.

Bopanna was visibly frustrated when I entered the lobby to meet him. People like him do not like being kept waiting. The policeman was in his late fifties. He tried to make up for his warm countenance by sitting in an arrogant posture, while two constables flanked him.

I wished him a good afternoon, to which he did not respond. He indicated a chair for me to sit at his table. I sat down and smiled at him. He frowned.

"What are you doing here?" he asked.

"Exercising my freedom of movement under Article 19 of the Constitution of India," I said with a smile. I was bent on answering his haughtiness with my smugness.

"Or are you trespassing into private property?"

"Is it a rhetorical question?" I asked.

"Answer me," he said, angrily.

"How can I answer when I do not understand what you mean?" I tried to evade the question.

"Why is your face swollen?"

"I punched myself in the face," I said, trying to insult him.

"Don't act smart," he shouted. The lobby manager looked around tentatively. "I have CCTV footage that you barged into Globosoft's office last week."

"I do not remember barging into any office. But since you have evidence, please follow the law and arrest me."

Bopanna glared at me. His constables looked at me menacingly. I glared back at them. They scowled back at me and something behind my back. I looked around to find Puwaiya scowling at them. The emaciated chap was shaking, and had to try real hard at looking fierce. I looked back at Bopanna, and smiled slyly.

"Would you like some coffee?" I asked.

"No," he retorted.

I waved at a waiter and asked him for coffee for Puwaiya and I, and water for the gentlemen in uniform. Bopanna realised that he could not overwhelm me merely with theatrics. So he changed tactics.

"My work here is to maintain balance. I don't like it when anyone disturbs that balance. Especially in software companies that contribute to jobs and economic development in my city," he said. "Palani Kumar wanted to press charges on you for impersonation, stealing and trespassing. I told him to wait. Compromise is the best way to end disputes."

"I had not trespassed. I requested the receptionist to let me meet the company's MD. Then, Palani Kumar, who was posing as chief of security, invited me inside. A person who I have impersonated can press charges of criminal impersonation. Who did I impersonate?" I asked.

"But you did steal, did you not?" Bopanna said.

"No, I did not. I ran away from there after they beat me up. See!" I said, pointing at my face.

"And you took a diary from Anbu Selvam," Bopanna said.

"If you think I am a thief, please file charges against me for stealing a diary," I said.

"There are many things the police can do other than filing charges," Bopanna said.

"Like?"

"Like… you will see when it happens. Better avoid it. Give me the diary and the matter stands resolved."

"I don't have any diary with me. If you want, I can purchase a diary and give it to you to buy peace. As for my swollen face, I have a dinner appointment with Bangalore's police commissioner. I will take up the issue at the dinner. I expect him to make a compromise between me and the gangsters at Globosoft."

"As if the commissioner has no other work but to have dinner with a felon," Bopanna said and chuckled.

"My friend Sanjay Mallya confirmed to me that the commissioner has no other work at dinner time today. We can only wait and find out if it's true," I said.

Bopanna's expression changed on hearing Mallya's name. Mallya must be pretty cosy with the commissioner, for his name lent a tone of authenticity to my claim.

"Oh, you know Mallya. He never mentioned you," Bopanna said.

"He never mentioned you to me either," I said and smirked.

"But he is a close friend. I did not know that. Mallya's friend is my friend," Bopanna said and stabbed into his smartphone. He was calling Mallya to confirm if I knew him.

"Hey Mallya," Bopanna spoke into the phone when it connected. "I am sitting with Mister Digyen Burmah here. Your name came up, so I thought of calling you."

Bopanna switched to Kannada and spoke with Mallya at length. Then he handed the phone to me. Mallya said, "Are you already dining with this bastard?"

"No, no," I said. After a pause, I continued, "No time for that now. I am enjoying coffee with Inspector Bopanna. We will meet at dinner time. Pick me up on your way."

I disconnected the call and placed the phone on the table. I stole a glance at the ACP to see his reaction when I referred to him as inspector. He had turned into a real teddy, and did not seem to take any offence.

"Mallya and I, we are thick," Bopanna said. "Since you are Mallya's friend, I should first apologise. I should not have been rude."

"Right. Now that we have put the initial awkwardness aside, I believe I can be frank with you."

"Yes, please!"

Bopanna signalled his men to leave. Puwaiya was still lingering behind me. I had started to enjoy his company, even though he stank of cheap liquor. I reluctantly asked him to sit at another table and wait for his coffee.

Bopanna took out my mobile phone which I had lost in Globosoft office, and handed it to me.

"I will go back and teach these idiots a lesson. They beat you and snatched your mobile phone. It's not done. Your phone is password protected, and all data is safe. I had to take out the SIM when Palani complained against you. We used the SIM to get your identity. I have checked: you have been hired by that fool Bhide to find his wife. Selvam is also searching for Bhide's wife. So you and Selvam are on the same page here. Better to join forces than fight among yourselves."

"Bhide asked me for help because the police were not ready to lodge a complaint to find his missing wife. His wife is missing for three months now, but no one seems to care," I said. "And he is not a client. He is a friend from my college days."

"How do we file a complaint? It's technically wrong to file FIR in the name of Swati Gupta. When Bhide approached the Domlur station, he did not give any identity of his wife – just photographs. He did not have any ID proof of the woman, no marriage certificate, nothing. He did not know any next of kin of Swati Gupta. He told the SHO[†] that the home minister of Bengal is Swati's father. So my SHO asked Bhide to furnish more details. In the meantime, Palani and Bhide had an understanding not to file an FIR. Bhide did not come back. Is it our mistake?"

"What about the forged PAN card and voter ID details?" I asked.

---

† SHO – Station House Officer

"I have heard rumours that the lady had submitted photocopies of forged identity cards to Globosoft when she joined the company. But no one at the company has formally filed a complaint. So we do not know. We don't even know if such a woman actually exists. The company does not step forward, and Bhide is mentally unstable. How do we allot resources to search for a ghost?"

I realised that Bopanna was legally correct for not accepting Bhide's complaint. It was not my place to allege that Bopanna was actually helping the Selvams locate Swati Gupta, without any proof. So I nodded my acceptance of his point.

"Why do you think Palani is searching for Swati Gupta?"

"Officially, no one at Globosoft has told me anything. But I could gather from Palani that software codes are the core assets of this company. These are trade secrets that the company protects from its competitors. It seems Swati has run away with some of these codes. It's a catch 22 situation for the company. If they lodge a complaint, they will have to reveal which software codes she has stolen. They will have to give us access to their database. It may further compromise their trade secrets."

"Makes sense," I nodded in mock agreement. "Now that you have enlightened me, I will join forces with Anbu Selvam and team."

I waved to the waiter and asked him to bill the coffee to my room, and then started to go. Bopanna stood up and came close to me. He whispered to me conspiratorially that I still had their diary. I should give it back to Anbu Selvam to maintain peace.

"But I don't have any diary. Did you see me carrying a diary in the CCTV feed?" I said. I remembered vividly that I had tucked the diary inside my jeans when I was leaving Globosoft office.

Bopanna hurried after me as I was proceeding towards the elevator. He requested me for my phone number, and typed it into his smartphone hurriedly. He made a last ditch effort, "We can ask Selvam for an offering in return for the diary. If you have a figure in mind, I can convince them to pay. Selvam is a practical man. He is also very generous."

"There is no hurry, is there? The priority now is to find Swati Gupta, take back the software codes, and rehabilitate her with Bhide. There is no hurry to cut deals. For now, send Palani to meet me," I said and entered the elevator. I could see the disappointment in Bopanna's expression as the elevator doors closed.

Upstairs, I packed the diary and sheets I had seized from Globosoft office in a plastic bag. I went to the toilet, turned off the valve supplying water to the commode, and drained the commode tank. I pasted the plastic bag to one side of the tank, and closed the tank.

9

Real Identity

Bidhya was planning to visit the Sinamangal slum area on an international assignment from India. But her husband, Partha was not comfortable with his wife going alone to the crime-infested slums on the banks of Bagmati river. She would be much safer if escorted by a driver in police uniform.

When Partha's car came back, Bidhya was surprised to find an armed constable accompanying the driver. Partha is the cautious type, thought Bidhya and smiled. But police escorts would only slow the intel she intended to collect on this day.

Arjun Gurung's stated address was a lane in Sinamangal slums. Shanty houses built in unauthorised areas usually do not carry house numbers. Bidhya needed local support to find Gurung and speak with him. Policemen are often seen as part of the exploiting 'establishment' in sub-cultures that develop in impoverished slums of Kathmandu. Police excesses against minor crimes add up to the image.

Luckily, Bidhya had the connections that only a housewife possesses. Her neighbour's maid's maternal family stayed in

Sinamangal. She had arranged for a teenager from the slum to escort her during her trip.

Bidhya stopped her husband's car outside Nobel Hospital on Sinamangal road and waited for the boy. The boy, Sudhir, soon arrived on a bicycle and parked it near the police car. Bidhya handed him packets of cookies and sweets she had purchased to give to Gurung. Partha had directed the constable to be with Bidhya at all times. He grudgingly allowed her to leave with Sudhir.

Sudhir took Bidhya through narrow roads into the heart of Sinamangal. Smell of rotting vegetables blended with foul smell from the open defecation areas by the riverside to give Bidhya a nausea. Sudhir looked back and chuckled.

"The nausea will go away in sometime, *kaki*," Sudhir said. He was eighteen years old and worked in a restaurant. He had dropped out in eighth grade.

On her way to Gurung's house, Bidhya could not help but notice that the kids in this area actually had no future. The air was dusty and pungent. Small shacks were built closely to house a large number of people.

Why would anyone leave the hinterland to live in such a polluted environment? Bidhya wondered.

She remembered how the Civil War between the Communist Party and National Government had hit the poor the most. They lost their livelihood and habitat. As village after village burnt, there was a mass exodus to Kathmandu, a city that offered a semblance of peace. Sinamangal swelled at the time and became the den that it presently is.

The Civil War ended when the two sides made peace. The People's Liberation Army merged with the National Army. But the civilians who lost their livelihood stayed back in Sinamangal. The general condition of this lot had dipped further over time.

▼

Arjun Gurung stayed in a one-room house on the first floor, in a narrow lane, with four grandchildren. The man was in his seventies. The eldest of his grandchildren was a twelve-year-old boy, while the youngest was a three-year-old girl. Two of the grandchildren were playing with other kids in the lane. Sudhir spoke with the twelve-year-old and gave him the cookies and sweets that Bidhya had brought.

Bidhya's presence in this locality was met with cold stares and gossips from the neighbourhood. Sudhir went upstairs to speak with Gurung. He came back in a while and said that Gurung was bedridden, and was in no mood to talk.

"It appears others have already come here asking about Preeti," Sudhir said. "The old man was terrified when I said a madam had come to speak with him."

"Okay. Can you get some tea? Is tea available nearby?"

Sudhir nodded. "What will you do kaki?"

"I will sit here, waiting for you. Get enough tea and biscuits, so we can offer others."

Sudhir went away to get tea. Bidhya found a broken chair in one corner. She sat there and took out Swati Gupta's photo in her smartphone. She intensely stared at the photograph that her client had sent her.

Her client had not briefed the entire case to her. He only said that a woman by the name of Swati Gupta was missing. She had married someone younger than her in age, and used him to swindle the company he was working in. She vanished on 7 April. Both husband and employer are looking for her. Her client Digyen Burmah was working at the husband's behest to find Swati Gupta.

The woman used to call Arjun Gurung regularly. Apparently, Swati looked like Preeti Gurung, and was probably her. Burmah found this incredible and difficult to believe. He kept saying that the woman did not look like a Nepali.

Bidhya tried to educate Burmah that Nepal is a potpourri of races. Most Nepalis have some Indian features and some oriental features in their looks. Many Gurung girls, like the Nepali actresses Jassita Gurung and Sanna Gurung, have negligible oriental features in their looks. The Bollywood heroine Manisha Koirala looks more Punjabi than Nepali.

Presently, a mid-aged woman called Saraswati approached Bidhya with a shy smile. She asked if Bidhya needed anything. Bidhya asked her if she could get a glass of water. The woman called one of the children playing with Gurung's grandchildren and ordered him to get a glass of water. The kid ran into one of the houses and came out with a glass of water.

Partha would never approve of Bidhya having water in this locality, even though he was not as mindful of cleanliness as Bidhya was. But Bidhya had to do it, to develop a rapport with Preeti's neighbourhood.

"What do you people want with Preeti? What could she have possibly done?"

This was the opening Bidhya was looking for. She convinced the woman that she was not one of the others and was there to help. She could sense suspicion in her tone. So, she considered it best to tell a version of the truth rather than a lie. She showed the photograph of Preeti sent by Burmah and explained that Preeti had vanished on 7 April without any prior notice. Her friends in Bangalore were worried about her. She worked for some dangerous people, who are also looking for her. So her friends hired a detective to investigate her disappearance. The detective had, in turn, hired her to coordinate with Preeti's family.

Saraswati opened up to Bidhya and explained Preeti's background to her. By the time Sudhir arrived with tea, few other women from the neighbourhood had joined. Preeti was quite popular in the neighbourhood, and everyone was concerned about her. Some women became teary while narrating Preeti's tragedies.

Many elderly women in the neighbourhood knew Preeti since her childhood. She had come to Sinamangal with her parents in the early 1990s from a village in the Birgunj region. Her father Arjun Gurung got a job as a mechanic in a nearby garage, while her mother worked as a maid in a colony close by.

Preeti was stunningly beautiful in her youth. No wonder she was popular in the entire Sinamangal, and many young men tried their luck on her. This was the time when new families were coming to Sinamangal to escape the Civil War.

One young man had come to Kathmandu from the Terai region and did odd jobs in a factory on the outskirts of Sinamangal. His name was Premnath. He met Preeti while enjoying an evening breeze by the Bagmati river, and instantly fell in love with her. Preeti discouraged him repeatedly, but he pursued his proposal doggedly. Premnath pampered her with gifts and dazzled her parents with his spendthrift habits. He claimed that his parents were well-to-do landlords loyal to the national government in the Terai region, but were in hiding because of threats from the Communist Party. While Preeti was not interested in him, he had managed to impress her parents. They convinced her to marry Premnath.

Premnath married Preeti and moved into Arjun Gurung's house. Premnath's duplicity was exposed just days after the wedding. He was knee deep in loans, which he spent in drinks and merrymaking. Arjun had to pay off the loans. It was then found that Premnath did not actually work in the factory, but loafed around it. He was good-for-nothing. Well, not actually good-for-nothing because she had four kids with him.

Preeti took up a sewing job in a boutique in the inner city. It fetched decent income for her. But many problems were brewing. Her mother died a couple of years after her wedding. Premnath turned alcoholic, and looked for every opportunity to take money to buy liquor. Arjun Gurung became ill and had to leave his job. He was later diagnosed with blood cancer. Preeti spent all her savings on his treatment. But the treatment was way costlier than her savings.

One fine day, Premnath left the family in this miserable situation. He took whatever money he could find in the house and vanished. That was three years ago. Preeti was pregnant with her fourth child at the time. Some people in the neighbourhood have seen him begging outside temples.

But Preeti did not make any effort to reach out to him. Her concerns were saving her father and educating the children. She somehow managed to make ends meet for a year.

She got an offer to do sewing in a boutique in Kolkata some fifteen months back. The boutique owner promised a salary of forty thousand Indian rupees and stay. Preeti has been working in Kolkata since then. At least, that's what she has made the neighbours believe. She was depositing thirty thousand rupees in the Indian bank account of a Sinamangal-based grocer, who gave the money to her father.

Preeti stayed in touch with her family on a daily basis. She called daily and spoke with her father and children. But her calls stopped on 7 April. Her phone was also not reachable. Arjun Gurung filed a complaint with the local police, and got in touch with few Nepalis staying in Kolkata. A youth from the neighbourhood now working in Kolkata filed a police case in Kolkata as well. But nothing came out of it.

Preeti had not given any contact in India. She was not in touch with any Nepali immigrant. She did not give any address or description of the boutique she worked in. Naturally, even the police could not help. And they would not go out of the way to find an inconsequential slum girl.

Days later, a lady came with an employee of the American embassy in Kathmandu to find Preeti. The lady looked Indian, but claimed that she was an American citizen. She said her NGO had chosen Preeti for a position in Kathmandu. She was desperate to get in touch with her. She cajoled Gurung for a long time, and apparently got frustrated when she could not extract anything from him. She gave veiled threats to Gurung after that.

Few local goons came the next day and took an ailing Gurung with them. Youth from the neighbourhood appealed to a local corporator to save Gurung from the goons. After the corporator threatened these goons, they dropped Gurung off two blocks away after keeping him for three days. Gurung confided with his neighbours that he was beaten badly in captivity. The same lady had interrogated him. She even threatened that she would chop off the hands of his grandchildren if he did not reveal where Preeti is.

Moved by this tragic tale, Bidhya asked Sudhir to call the constable and her husband's driver into the lane. She revealed her husband's identity and assured the concerned neighbours that police would help the family more diligently now onwards.

Bidhya sent the assembled women with the constable upstairs to meet Gurung and assure him of all support from the police. She used this opportunity to talk with Saraswati in private. She asked her to describe the lady who had come to meet Gurung. Saraswati described the lady as posh. She was five feet and six inches tall, had a slim waistline and long, straight, dark hair. She had a dusky complexion. Oval face with high cheekbones and pouty lips. Bidhya typed notes into her smartphone, although she realised that this revelation would not lead her to Preeti.

Bidhya asked Saraswati if she could throw some light on the person in India who recruited Preeti. She shrugged and said that Preeti was evasive about her job offer from Kolkata.

Bidhya wanted to take the narrative on face value. But she knew that the narrative built by these well-meaning neighbours did not add up. A woman does not usually land a job in India without going through some known contact.

How did Preeti land this job in Kolkata? Who helped her in getting it? Was it someone in the slum? Was it someone at work?

There was no use pushing these people, for it would make them suspicious about her motives.

Bidhya took out a business card and gave it to Saraswati. "Call me if you recall anything that can help us find Preeti. I feel she is in big trouble," Bidhya said with utmost sincerity. "Together, we can help her and her kids," Bidhya added, to instil a sense of duty in Saraswati.

▼

On her way back, Bidhya tipped a thousand rupees in Indian currency to Sudhir, and gave him another two thousand rupees with instructions to get chocolates and groceries for Gurung and his family a day later.

She was confident that Saraswati would get back to her in a couple of days with a lead.

10

Eureka Moment

Why would a software company dabble in Hawala? That too, a software company that got its revenues from American customers. Was Globosoft sending money to someplace outside India? Was it receiving money from someplace outside India? Where did the money come from? Where did it go?

Anbu Selvam's diary showed me that the group maintained a bunch of offshore bank accounts in tax havens, where money was rotated and layered. And there were some clerics running madrasas in Tamil Nadu and Karnataka who Selvam was paying in cash.

I could safely presume that Globosoft was not using Hawala in its regular business transactions. Hawala was used in regular trade and commerce during ancient and medieval times. Colonial rulers also used it, but they drove Hawaladars underground. After Independence, Hawala has principally been used by migrants to send money back to their family in India.

Shortly after Partition in 1947, India and Pakistan developed frosty relations and banned all monetary and trade transactions.

Hawala was then used by families split by partition to transfer money across the border. Hawala finance slowly developed from this time to cover all countries where Indians migrated in good numbers. When workers from Kerala went to Gulf countries, a bustling Hawala channel developed on this route. When enterprising young men from Punjab landed in Canada and US, they needed a cheap route to send money home. Hawaladars crept up to service these migrants.

Many of these migrants are from an extremely poor background, and family members are solely dependent on remittances made by the migrant worker. This makes remittance a crucial responsibility of the migrant for sustaining his family.

Unfortunately, a large number of such emigrants are illegal and undocumented. Informal channels are their only option. Legal migrants use the Hawala channel when international banks have limited financial reach in remote areas of their home country. Hawala networks have unparalleled reach, and are quite fast. Hawaladars develop personal, face-to-face relations with the client. The Hawaladar is usually a first- or second-generation immigrant and is well known in localities dominated by ethnic migrants.

Hawala transfer is cheaper for the migrant than banks because physical movement of cash does not happen. There is a group of Hawaladars sitting overseas and a group sitting in India. Overseas Hawaladars send poor migrants' money to Indian Hawaladars. Indian Hawaladars also send money to overseas Hawaladars. This way, they adjust their 'cash in' with 'cash out', and do not have to physically move money. So technically, no one sends money physically across Indian borders.

But whose money do Indian Hawaladars send to overseas Hawaladars?

The trend in Hawala finance indicates that the clerics give cash to Globosoft. Globosoft sends the cash offshore through the Hawala route, and parks the money in tax havens. But the theory just does not add up. It does not give me an 'eureka!' moment. Why will madrasas use a middleman to hide their money abroad? They can directly liaison with a Hawaladar. Why will different madrasas belonging to different sects and Islamic schools of thought use the same middleman to hide their money abroad?

More importantly, madrasas do not need to hide their money abroad. Educational intitutes are legally registered as charitable or religious trusts. The tax department allows such trusts to accept public donation, and does not impose tax on them.

So why will they take the trouble of hiding the money abroad?

I rejected the theory and looked for an alternate one.

I took out the financials of Globosoft and reviewed them. Globosoft's finances were themselves abnormal, but did not throw any hint. The company has been operating at negligible profit margins. It does not develop any software. It gets software contracts from the US and further sub-contracts them to boutique companies in Bangalore and Pune. In a way, it is a shell company. It should at least retain a part of its revenue, for being the company that sealed the deal with the foreign clients.

But it does not. It keeps only nominal amount to cover expenses and pays the rest of fees received from clients to its sub-contractors. It collaborates with few researchers at IITs to come up with pathetic patent proposals. Its patents are useless and can never be commercialised.

While going through Globosoft's finances, I realised that I had overlooked its sister concerns. There was a charitable trust, Malabar Children Education Society, which Selvam's wife managed. I gave its key figures a relook. The Trust received handsome amounts from donors in Dubai between 2008 and 2014. Dubai is a red flag. The Trust had received more than a hundred crores in funding in 2014.

But it had not utilised the funds for any charitable activity. Rather, it donated the funds to other NGOs, educational institutions and orphanages. In a way, the Trust was behaving like the company. While Globosoft took contracts and further sub-contracted the work, the Trust took donations and further donated the funds.

But trusts are more troublesome than companies. Globosoft had sub-contracted the work to genuine software companies. These sub-contractors ultimately did testing and coding work for the American clients. What about the Trust? It received huge monies from a tax haven and just distributed the money.

I tried to profile some of the organisations that the Malabar Children Education Society had donated to. And then, all of a sudden, I came upon my eureka moment.

The Trust brought foreign money into India and paid influential clerics in the form of donation. The Trust could not use formal banking route to bring foreign money after 2014. So, it had no option but to bring in money through the Hawala channel.

The theory made sense. *But why did the Trust not continue getting funds through banking channels?* To understand this, I skimmed through the website of Foreign Contribution Regulation Act (FCRA). FCRA approvals are given by the Home Ministry. No charitable organisation can bring donations into the country without FCRA approval. Malabar Children Education Society had FCRA approval till 2014. The approval was withdrawn in 2015.

The reason was that some other NGOs along with this Trust lost their license merely because they could not demonstrate how the foreign donation was being used for charity. The Trust did not conduct any charitable activity. Selvam used the Trust to receive funds from Dubai, and distributed the funds among domestic NGOs. Then it lost its FCRA license. But Selvam had to get the money into India anyway. So he used the Hawala route to get the donation into India.

Now that's a theory I can work with.

11

The Interrogation

Palani Kumar arrived at the hotel just three hours after I had asked ACP Bopanna to send him. It seemed Selvam was desperate to get his diary back.

I wanted to frustrate Palani with a long wait before I started my interrogation. I made Palani wait at the reception for about half an hour. Then, I phoned Puwaiya and asked him if he knew Tamil. He told me that Tamil was his mother tongue. I asked Puwaiya to talk with Palani in a local language and extract as much information as he can. I secretly wished that Puwaiya would inform Palani that he is Don Mutthapa Rai's man.

I did not have anything particular to do in my hotel room. I wanted to frustrate Palani and pump up his emotions before starting my interrogation.

I took the time to talk with Saby Biswas and brief him about the case. He is the best expert on Hawala operators I know. I requested him to track Ramakrishna Kedia and find a way to extract information from him on what exactly happened that day when Swati Gupta met him. I emailed him a detailed report, mentioning the facts and my inferences after analysing the CDR data. Then I went down to the lobby and peeped around. It was post noon, and the swimming pool area was deserted. It would be the best place for me to interrogate Palani.

I went to the lobby, but did not find Palani or Puwaiya. I looked around, and found them drinking whiskey in the bar. They were animatedly chatting, like old friends.

Who served whiskey to Puwaiya in a five-star hotel? Can he even afford it?

I stood at their table and glared at Puwaiya. He understood my displeasure and made a lousy effort to get up. He was completely wasted, probably had greedily gulped down some costly scotch that Palani offered him. Palani invited me to join them at the table, but I ignored him. I asked Puwaiya to wrap up and bring Palani Kumar to the swimming pool area, and went out of the bar.

I sat in a corner in the poolside porch and waited for the two drunks. Puwaiya had washed away all my plans with his free liquor. While I wanted Palani to feel a sense of awe and fear, Puwaiya had made him as comfortable as he could get.

Puwaiya and Palani Kumar joined me in a moment. Palani bowed reverentially and sat across me, while Puwaiya stood behind me. He kept shaking.

"Bopanna *sar* asked me to meet you and say sarry. I am sarry sar for what happened that day. My MD also sarry sar. We feel very bad sar," Palani said.

I kept looking at him. The interrogator should usually keep quiet at the start, so as to get all information that the subject wants to voluntarily give. Such information is usually false.

"We misunderstood sar. We are on the same team here. We will join forces to find Swati Gupta," Palani said and smiled at Puwaiya. I kept silent.

"Anbu Selvam also wants to meet you sar, and say sarry."

We looked silently at each other for a few more moments. The bastard was not ready to say anything by himself.

"Why are you looking for Swati Gupta so desperately?" I asked.

"She stole software codes from Globosoft office," Palani said.

"What software codes? You guys sub-contract all coding work you get. You do not develop any software yourself."

"The sub-contractors share code with us. Trust me sar, she took our software codes."

"Then why was Selvam asking me about the 'money' when I was posing as Swati's lawyer?"

Palani looked uncomfortable. "She also took some money from our MD. But that is MD's personal matter. Nat company's matter."

"How much money?" I asked.

"Some five lakhs, I am told."

"Look Mr Palani, whether we are on the same side or not will be decided in the next few minutes. I will decide based on your answers if I can trust you. Correct?"

Palani nodded.

"When did you last meet Ramakrishna Kedia?"

Palani was taken aback on hearing the name. "Who?"

"I will not repeat myself. Answer my question, or the diary will reach the income tax department within the next hour."

"Boss has sent me to meet Kedia to pick documents a few times. I think I met him last in January," Palani said softly.

"Good. That's progress. What business does he have with Kedia?"

"I do nat know his business sar. Some company matter! I only handle security."

"Last chance. What *business* does your boss have with Hawaladar Kedia?"

"He… he… sometimes needs money for expenses…so… so… his wife is American citizen… she stays in America… she sends money to him."

"How much money did you bring from Kedia in January?"

"Five… six lakhs," Palani said, this time more shakily.

"Now tell me what happened that day when Swati disappeared."

"Sar," Palani bellowed, almost in tears, "I do nat know. I have to ask boss."

"You are lying," I said angrily.

"Please sar! Let me ask boss. I am only a small employee. I know nothing. I will bring my boss."

"Let me tell you what I think. You and Swati conspired against Selvam and stole crores brought by him from offshore accounts through the Hawala route."

Palani's eyes widened in amazement and fear. "It is nathing like that. Your story is pure fiction."

"Where is Swati?"

"I do nat know sar."

"Where have you hidden her?"

"No sar." Palani shook his head vigorously.

"Remember those days when Swati was working for your MD? What were you speaking with her in SMS chats all night? And why did you call her multiple times on the day she disappeared?"

"Sar you have got all wrong. I was looking for boss. His number was switched off, and Swati was in Mumbai… but how do you know sar? Have you seen her call records?"

"I ask the questions, you give the answers. I guess Bopanna has already given you Swati's CDR. I bet you have not told your boss about your midnight messaging with Swati, nor about the frequent calls you made to her."

"What do I have to hide sar? I have to report names of security staff on duty daily to boss. Boss wanted me to send reports to Swati. He gave her all control. What can I do? I used to message her guard names and duty times daily. No hanky panky sar."

"Then give me your smartphone. Let me check."

"No sar," Palani bellowed.

"Or admit that you swindled Anbu Selvam."

"What are you saying sar? My life is devoted to the cause sar. I am committed. Money means nathing to me sar." Palani was agitated by now.

"What cause?" I asked

"Sar my boss was close to Swati. I knew they slept together whenever they went on tour… but I had no affair with Swati."

How much money did you pick from Kedia in January? Tell me the truth."

"I do nat know sar. I will have to ask boss."

"Last chance. How much money did Swati take from Kedia?"

Palani stood up and said, "Sar! Let me speak with boss. He knows best. He will give all the answers. I will go now." Palani folded his hands in obeisance and hurriedly left.

I turned to Puwaiya and indicated to him to take Palani's seat.

"So, you two are fast friends now?" I asked him sarcastically.

Puwaiya blushed and said, "We have like interests in movies."

"Well, he is the enemy. That bastard and his friends and his boss beat me up in their office last week. I sent you to extract information from him, and all you did was drink and discuss movies?"

"No sir, I extracted information. Easy to extract information from a drunk man."

"Oh. And what information did you extract? The movies he likes?"

"No sir. That man Anbu Selvam not his boss. His boss a lady from America. He calls her Lokka. Palani respects Lokka very much. Lokka also Anbu's boss."

I was dumbfounded. "Go on!"

"Anbu had affair with an employee. What Palani told you also. The girl cheated them. You created more problems last week. So Lokka is here to sort matters."

"Anything about the girl Anbu was having affair with?"

"They are in search of the girl. She might have left the country. She accessed her facebook profile from Kuala Lumpur two weeks back, and again three days back. Bopanna and cyber police are helping them find her."

Puwaiya had impressed me with decent leads.

"Would you like one more drink at the bar?"

12

The Knight Rider

The seventeen hundred-kilometres-long border between Nepal and India is one of the busiest human trafficking gateways in the world.

More than ten thousand women are trafficked from Nepal every year through its porous border with India. Aspiring migrant workers, women in the adult entertainment industry and girls from rural areas are most vulnerable to trafficking.

As Bidhya had guessed, Preeti's neighbour Saraswati phoned her soon after she left the Sinamangal slum area. Saraswati knew facts about Preeti's life that she could not reveal in front of the neighbours. Preeti had become gloomy after years of financial troubles. She was always short of money to spend on her father's continued treatment. Her children remained impoverished all the time. She was the only earning member of the family.

Preeti often compared herself with friends who got married and led a better life. Even though she was popular and prettiest of the lot, fortune did not smile on her.

Saraswati used to lend her small change to buy daily supplies. But one day, four years ago, Preeti returned all the money she had loaned from Saraswati. She returned loans she had taken from others in the neighbourhood too. She later confided to Saraswati that she was working part time in a dance bar in Thamel, the busiest commercial and tourist market of Kathmandu.

Preeti got an offer to perform in a dance bar by the name of Knight Rider in Thamel. But there was always a risk that young men from her locality would come to the bar to drink, and find her dancing there. So she preferred a more dangerous role – high end prostitution. If any guest in the dance bar solicited sex, the bar would send him to a room with Preeti.

A friend of Preeti's husband Premnath work as a Himalayan trekking guide in the Thamel area. One day, he saw Preeti coming out of a client's hotel room. He informed Premnath. Naturally, Premnath was furious, and frequent fights broke out between the couple since then. Then, came the news that Preeti was pregnant. Premnath got engulfed in doubts that the child Preeti was carrying was not his. He drank with a vengeance, and got completely wasted. Preeti discontinued her part-time job at the Knight Riders, but this did not satisfy Premnath. One day, just like that, he left home.

Preeti was stricken by both grief and guilt. Saraswati claimed that she was the only one in the locality to whom Preeti confided her conundrum. She needed the financial freedom that a job at the Knight Riders gave her. At the same time, guilt ate into her.

Since then, the idea of going to India for work took root in her mind. She had heard stories of girls who made quick dough in India and came back to a life of financial security. She was looking for such a scheme.

And she did get such an offer around this time. A tourist from India who had hired her services for a night, called her with a request to meet. Preeti only said that he paid for the entire night, but did not engage with her physically. He talked with her all night, and took her number.

The tourist gave her an offer when they met. The offer was to go with him to India and work on a heist. He would incur all her expenses and send a regular stipend to her family. The heist would need one to two years of preparation. If the heist became successful, she could take her share and go back to Nepal. Her share, he promised, would be at least fifty lakh rupees in Indian currency.

The tourist had explained to her that secrecy was of paramount importance in this mission. Saraswati felt it was risky to take a stranger on face value. But Preeti seemed convinced by the dream this tourist showed her. She left for India leaving behind three kids and an infant.

▼

The story made sense now. The version Preeti's neighbours narrated had not made sense. Saraswati provided the missing pieces to Preeti's story. Bidhya was convinced that this tourist would reveal all remaining secrets of the case.

Bidhya also realised that it was indeed difficult to identify this 'Tourist'. First, tourists are difficult to nail. Moreover, Preeti serviced many clients during her time in the Knight Rider. Pimps soliciting customers in dance bars often do not maintain records. Even when they do, they destroy the records after the work is done.

A person who has gone to Nepal to look for a pawn for a heist would be careful enough not to use a number registered under his name. The Tourist paid in cash. He kept paying a stipend to Preeti while she was in India, but this too was in cash.

Bidhya got in touch with the Thamel Police Station through her husband. She wanted to explore the possibility that a pimp at the workplace could give some description of the Tourist who recruited Preeti. A sub-inspector in the station was charged with the responsibility to enquire and report to Bidhya.

But the Knight Rider did not give many clues to Bidhya. The matter was four years old, and the staff had changed in this time. The sub-inspector found that all waiters at Knight Rider doubled up as pimps and solicited the bar's customers. Many of the waiters who worked four years back had left. Others remembered Preeti (she went by the name of 'Pinky' at the bar), but could not recall any specific customer who they found suspicious.

The bar manager informed the sub-inspector that a posh lady with dusky complexion had visited his office enquiring about the same girl sometime in April. She was accompanied by Gurkha guards, who she had probably hired from a local security agency. The guards were armed, and had dropped references before turning up.

So the bar manager had cooperated with them. The lady took down details of all waiters who worked during Pinky's time in the bar. She went around the locality and asked every vendor who owned CCTV if they stored CCTV footage from four years ago.

The Knight Rider was not exactly a dead end. Bidhya could pursue leads with the waiters who left the bar since Preeti's time there. She could also check with hotels in the area. But the Indian client had hired her only for basic enquiries, not in-depth sleuthing. He was in a hurry to get to the bottom of the matter, because the company Swati (a.k.a. Preeti) worked in had a head start of at least two months. So, Bidhya compiled all her notes and sent a report to Burmah the next morning itself.

Bidhya concluded her report with the observation that a woman who made great sacrifices for her family would not stop all communication for such a long period. It is against a mother's nature.

Even while entering her conclusions in the report, Bidhya was clear that Swati Gupta alias Preeti Gurung alias Pinky was dead.

13

The Dream

On Thursday, Sneha's phone call woke me up four hours past midnight, before it was even morning. She had a restless night and could not sleep. She launched into a diatribe on how I had forgotten her after leaving for Bangalore. I partly slept through the diatribe and tried to convince her that I missed her every moment.

"At least tell something I can believe. After marrying you for three years now, I at least know when you are lying and when you are just exaggerating."

"Do you know why I am out here? Do you know what I am going through in the heat of July? Well, news for you. You kept pestering me to take up an assignment. I was good at home. But you kept accusing me of watching Netflix at home." I paused for dramatic effect, and continued, "What could I do? I had to take up this assignment and toil in this heat."

"Is it hot in Bangalore? But Bangalore must be having pleasant weather, no," Sneha said. Her talking about the weather is a sign that she is ready to reconcile. "I know what my *sona baccha* is going through all alone. I only felt worried because I had an ominous dream. My intuition says something bad is going to happen."

"Intuitions are irrational, Sneha," I reproached.

"But they are not irrational Digi. You know that… you have seen how my intuitions have come true."

"You fit events to match your interpretations, Sneha."

"Not everyone thinks rationally like robots and you," Sneha said. Her tone was again turning confrontational. I changed tact and asked her what her intuitions were. Proving a point to a wife is, after all, a pyrrhic victory and comes at a great cost.

"An evil demon has set her eyes on you, but she deceives you. You cannot see that she is *Chandi.*"

"But Chandi is a goddess. She kills demons, if I am not wrong," I argued.

"No, Durga took on the Chandi form to kill demons. Only Durga in Chandi form is a goddess. Other Chandis are evil."

"All evil women in this world are thirsting for your husband, the personification of Rudra on earth. The world indeed is a dangerous place for you, doll," I said in mock sympathy.

She did not take it in the right spirit. Angrily, she shot her warning: "If I find you loafing around some woman there, I will pull her eyes out. And it will end badly for you."

Sneha ended the call on a bitter note. Her purpose had been served – instil fear of the omniscient wife in me. I was married long enough to know that Sneha's intuitions usually came true. I went back to sleep with great expectations of exciting encounters ahead.

▼

I woke up again at around nine in the morning and freshened up. I put on a fresh pair of jeans and a polo neck T-shirt, and went down to the hotel's buffet hall for breakfast. I found Puwaiya loitering around the hotel lobby and took him with me to the buffet hall.

I got a call from Nidhi while we were having breakfast. I hoped she was not the demoness my wife allured to earlier in the day, while attending to her call. She informed me that it was a work-from-home day for her, so she could come over to assist me in my investigation.

"And how will you assist in the investigation?" I asked.

"I don't know. You tell me."

"Some updates for you first. Swati Gupta is a mother of four kids. She is a Nepali MILF."

"What's a MILF?" she asked.

'That's not important. Swati Gupta's real name is Preeti Gurung. She seems to be an ordinary woman from Kathmandu. I have a person on the ground investigating her background and how she came to India.'

"So we get her if we know who brought her to India?"

"Yes. No. Maybe," I said, thoughtfully.

"What yes, no? Bhide is becoming restless. Anbu Selvam called him to his chamber the other day and rebuked him for hiring you. Bhide now acknowledges that Selvam is up to something. And the home minister – he wants to know when you will question him."

"You do understand that the home minister angle is purely illogical, don't you? I have already tracked the real father of Swati Gupta to Nepal."

"I do, but how do I make him understand?" she said helplessly.

"Confront him. Explain to him that he is being stupid. Now we have evidence also. I have Swati Gupta's application for an N Cell mobile connection in Nepal. Her name in the form is Preeti Gurung. I have located her house in a slum in Kathmandu. She has a family there. All that she told Bhide were white lies."

"I will tell all that to him. But you need to understand that he is mired by love. He is concerned about her safety."

"The facts I am giving you have nothing to do with love. He has to only apply his mind rationally to conclude that he was used to dupe his boss," I said, getting annoyed.

"Not everybody can be rational like you, or a computing machine… Humans have emotions. They think from their heart. They can't understand you, you can't understand them," Nidhi reproached.

I gulped down some coffee and took a big bite of the blueberry muffin.

"You are right," I said. "We need to find Swati Gupta first. That's the brief Bhide has given me. He foots my bill, who am I to complain. I need to find Swati. I will keep billing Bhide till I find her."

"You got any leads?" she enquired.

"Yes. Swati Gupta has accessed her facebook profile multiple times in the last two weeks, from IP addresses in Kuala Lumpur. I checked out her facebook profile. Just as Bhide had said, she has not uploaded any photograph of her face on Facebook. Bhide met her the first time through this profile."

'So you will go to Kuala Lumpur?'

"And do what?" I retorted. "We are missing critical clues. To find Swati, we need to identify her associates first. I will get more insight once my freelancer in Kathmandu files a report. Swati is definitely propped up by an insider. He may be Anbu Selvam, or his brother, or one of their cronies, or Kedia – a Hawala agent who regularly serviced Selvam – or someone else at their office. We need to skim clues from the gaps in our knowledge. Meet Bhide and take a detailed briefing from him on Swati's habits and her daily routine. Talk to his colleagues who had interacted with Swati. Can you do that for me?"

"Yes boss! I am on it," she said, excitedly. "Just one question. How can you suspect Anbu Selvam as the insider helping her? His money has been lost, right?"

"Apparently he is not the boss. The boss is a lady. I am still grappling with the facts. It's highly possible that he swindled the boss."

"Gotcha. Then I will go to Bhide's place now," Nidhi said and disconnected her call.

▼

Puwaiya had brought a yellow-coloured Yamaha FZS bike. I sat behind him and gave him directions as he drove me to the Globosoft office. I gave him random driving directions as I conducted a thorough recce of the office. There was no pan shop or shanty outside the office to buy tea from. The closest place for tea was a Chaayos outlet on the ground floor of an adjacent building.

I took Puwaiya to the Chaayos outlet and ordered tea. Puwaiya was slightly disappointed on seeing the tea. He probably wondered why we were having tea here when the beverage was being served in the buffet breakfast.

After taking two sips from my tea, I went to the counter and asked the waiter how long he had been working in the outlet. He said that he was working there for about a year.

"I need some information on this outlet. Is there someplace we can freely talk?" I asked.

"Wait for me behind the outlet. I am coming out in two minutes," the waiter said.

He was out in two minutes.

"Actually, I needed some information," I said, and placed a five hundred rupee note in his shirt pocket. Then I took out a photo of Swati Gupta and showed it to him.

"You recognise her?"

"Yes. She used to come here for tea. She worked in the Globosoft office."

"I know. But she has not been here lately," I said. "She is missing. And I need to find her. Who was she coming here with?"

"She used to come here daily after office. She talked over the phone for over an hour daily. She would not order any food or beverage, just sit in a corner and talk on the phone. Other times, she used to come here with a body builder fellow."

"Can you describe this body builder fellow?" I enquired.

"Well, he was tall, dark in complexion. His hair was unkempt, the kind which grows here and there because the person has not combed."

"Is it this person?" I asked him, showing a Facebook photograph of Palani Kumar.

"Yes, that's him." His eyes gleamed.

"Were they close?" I asked.

"Yes, appeared so. She used to be happy around him. They had lots to talk about. Sometimes they sat for hours together."

14

The Demoness

Bidhya had sent me a report of her enquiries by email, and had scheduled a Skype chat at five in the evening. I read her report and shared a gist with Nidhi.

Nidhi: So this tourist is behind the fraud?

Me: Appears so.

Nidhi: How do we identify him?

Me: Globosoft's goons are searching for him for months now. I don't think they have located him yet.

Me: Have you reached Bhide's place?

Nidhi: I started late. About to reach his place.

Me: Inform him about what my freelancer has found in Kathmandu. She has sent photographs of Swati's locality and her house. No need to confront him, just inform him what we have found.

Nidhi: Will do.

Me: One more thing.

Me: I have a suspect. Remember Palani Kumar?

Nidhi: The security guy who beat you in Globosoft office?

Me: I think Swati had an affair with him as well.

Nidhi: My god!

I connected with Bidhya at five in the evening. She had called me from her dining room. She explained her findings in greater detail to me, and concluded that finding the tourist was the key to cracking the case.

"Finding the Tourist is not my brief. Swati Gupta married a simpleton a year back. He is madly in love with her. She made him believe in a cock-and-bull story. My brief is to find Swati. If she has been kidnapped, or if she is in any problem, I am required to assist her."

"Okay. So, for all we know, she might be dead. Maybe you can tell her husband about the kids and her father. They are in dire condition."

"But what will the husband do if they are in dire condition?" I asked her.

"He may decide to adopt them or something."

"Why will he adopt them?" This lady did not make any sense.

"Because they are family. He is her husband. They are his responsibility."

I could not control my laughter at the proposition. "He is not her husband. She fooled him. Remember? She defrauded him."

"Not she, the Tourist defrauded him. He committed fraud with her as well as the husband. If her husband loves her as much as you said, it means they had a healthy married relationship."

"She *fooled him* into marrying her. She cheated on him by sleeping with his boss. How did they have a healthy married relationship?"

"She was *made to do that* – by the Tourist. If he could sustain love in marriage for a year, it means they had a healthy relationship."

"I am also married, Bidhya," I chuckled. "I don't need this dissemination of funda on relationship. Anyway, I will inform the husband about the condition her family is in. Since she has robbed someone's money and has to be on the run, he should take care of her family."

"She is not on the run. She is *dead*!" she emphasised.

"That's one possibility. How can you be sure that she is dead?"

"That is what happens to women who have been trafficked for crime. The Tourist was extra careful not to leave any trace when he trafficked her. You think he will let her live after the heist on Globosoft? She is a loose end that Globosoft's goons would use to get to him. She has to be silenced, and she was silenced."

"Then there is news for you. Swati has accessed her Facebook profile in Kuala Lumpur recently." I did not have to tell this fact to Bidhya; as a freelancer, she needs to be informed on a need-to-know basis only. I told this bit to her on an impulse, just to prove her wrong.

"That can't be true," Bidhya whispered.

"Remember Indrani Mukherjee? The woman from Assam who was arrested on charges of killing her own daughter? I can't still believe what the police have alleged against her.

What I understand is that crime is committed by deviants, not conformists. Preeti Gurung is a deviant. She engaged in prostitution for financial security. Her husband left her in disgust… and she did not try to get him back home."

"Is that her real profile or the profile of Swati Gupta?" Bidhya asked.

"Preeti Gurung does not have a profile anywhere. I had checked the day you sent me scans of her application forms for NCell. Preeti Gurung is not on any social network. So it's Swati Gupta's profile," I updated her.

"Why would she access her fake Facebook profile after the job is done?"

"Maybe to contact someone in her friends' list. Maybe she was bored. Maybe she actually loves her husband, and wanted to check on him. Possibilities are immense," I surmised.

"No doubt there are remote possibilities. But it is also possible that the Tourist, who used her, actually ran her Facebook profile. He is the mastermind, remember? He is trying to distract the goons looking for him. Also, consider the fact that Preeti's father was kidnapped by Globosoft's goons. He was tortured. He is ailing from cancer, and there is no money for his treatment. She has a three-year-old daughter who is being brought up by her siblings, because there is no one to take care of her. If Preeti was alive, she would have showed up… or sent money through someone to help," Bidhya was convinced with her theory.

'But if Preeti knows that the company's hired goons are looking for her in Nepal, she would lay low. If she gets exposed in Kathmandu, she would lose her life and all the money she has looted. Ultimately, it's a cost-benefit analysis,' I rationalized the situation.

"A mother never does cost-benefit analysis of her kids' lives," Bidhya said. She was furious now.

"The rational decision anyone will take in Preeti's place would be to lay low till the goons give up," I suggested.

"Exactly! That's a rational decision, not an emotional one. Mothers do not make rational decisions when they carry a child in their womb for nine months, nor when they take pains for years to raise the child. Even emotional men do not understand the depth of a mother's attachment. And you are too..."

She stopped short of saying that I am too rational. I pursed my lips up, raised an eyebrow, and acted as if I gave a serious thought to what she was saying.

"What I meant was her husband should know that she is dead and her family is in distress," Bidhya said.

▼

It was half-past six by the time my video call with Bidhya ended. I rushed off to the hotel's gym for a short workout. I took a quick shower after the workout and served myself a peg of whiskey from the minibar.

Later, I went down to the bar. It was almost empty, it being a weekday. A lone woman was sitting on one end of the bar table, sipping a bluish yellow mocktail. She was dressed in a white spaghetti top with a jacket, and silky white parallels.

I took a seat on the other end of the bar table and ordered a bourbon whiskey on the rocks. I stole a glance and instantly recognised the woman. *I know who she is*. The immediate question that came to my mind was: has she come for me? She did not seem to notice me at the bar table. It's highly plausible that she had come here for a drink. This is the only five-star hotel close to Globosoft office.

I ordered chicken nachos and went on with my eating and drinking noisily. I intentionally ignored her and fiddled on my smartphone.

"How are the nachos?" she asked me after sometime.

"Manageable," I said. "They make it better at the Irish bar in Indiranagar. Here, try it out." I offered her my plate, from which she took out a small piece and nibbled on it.

She had definitely come to meet me. But why put on the act? I wondered. *Does she know that I know who she is?* I ignored her and kept gulping my whiskey.

"You waiting for someone?" she asked.

"Nope! Just having a drink, and enjoying Bangalore's clement weather." I looked at her up close and realised that she had sharp features that were not discernible in the LinkedIn and web photographs I had seen.

"I got stood up," she said and pouted. Her lips were pulpy and jutted out of her oval face. She had long, shiny hair that went down to her waist. She definitely did not know that I knew who she was.

Was she trying to seduce me to wean away her diary? I was definitely game.

"Next drink is on me," she said and came over to my side of the bar table. She indicated to the bartender to refill her mocktail and my drink.

"Thank you. But bourbons do not quench my thirst," I said and threw a dirty look through her jacket at her cleavage. Any woman would take offence to such a lewd pass from a stranger. But she chose to ignore it with an encouraging smile.

"What kind of idiot does not show up to meet a princess?" I asked her. I had to play along, if I dreamt of tasting those breasts. Questions of morality kept pestering a remote part of my brain, while I concentrated the rest of my cognitive energy on this beauty, and her booty.

"Well, I don't mind. It was a date fixed by an aunt. I wasn't so eager to meet this guy. I was more looking forward to a chance encounter."

"Digyen Burmah at your service, your majesty."

"I am no majesty. Just a little girl."

"What do you do, little girl?"

"I am an artist. What about you?"

"I solve problems. You will not know until you try me out."

She made a face. "Seriously, that's your pick up line?"

"I have been out of touch."

"You do know who I am, don't you? So why were you playing around?"

"You were being sportive, Misses Roopalaxmi Sivanarayanan. Quite a name for a hot chick. I hear you got a husband who works two blocks away," I said. "By the way, how does it work? How did the midget bag something like this? And how does he handle this?"

"Information for you! No one bags Roopa. No one can handle Roopa."

"So what is it you have with Anbu Selvam?"

"He is a good worker. My father and Anbu enjoyed a master-servant relationship. He continues to be an employee in my company."

I took leisurely swigs of my whiskey and studied Roopa from top to bottom.

"Your nickname is Lokka, right? You were enquiring around for Preeti Gurung in Kathmandu. You picked up her ailing father and tortured him."

"I don't enjoy doing that. My company was tricked," she said non-chalantly.

"And what was the trickery?"

"Lets go to your room. You can study my figure better, and we can speak in privacy."

Roopa was bossy and assertive. I yielded to her directions pretty soon and escorted her up to my room.

Once inside my room, Roopa took off her jacket and laid down on the sofa. She put her legs on the coffee table and asked me to make her tea. I obediently did as I was told. I even asked her how much sugar she wanted. I could not believe myself!

Roopa tasted the tea, grimaced disgustingly and spit it out.

"Where is the diary?"

"Why are you people so desperate to get it back?"

"I will be frank with you. It has company secrets. That idiot Anbu could not hold his pants and fucked that prostitute from Nepal. She robbed company money. As if that was not bad enough, Anbu lost the one thing he was not supposed to lose – the diary."

"A third mistake – they beat up Digyen Burmah."

"True. You have still not healed," Roopa said and came over. She wrapped me between her legs and sat on me. Then she caressed the swollen parts of my face. I could feel her silicone boobs breathe against my chest. A part of my body got a blood rush and involuntarily woke up. If Roopa felt it, she did not react.

"Forget what happened earlier," Rupa said. "Now you deal with me. I don't want this to unravel further. Give the diary back, and state your price."

"What are those names in the diary?"

"What do you think?" she asked.

"You used a Trust as a front to bring funds into India. The money was paid to few clerics and leaders from a minority community. Then you lost your FCRA license, because allegedly you did not conduct any charity. But you so desperately need the money here that you brought it in cash through the Hawala route. But what was the desperation? The clerics impart free education, which is a charitable act. Why pay local community leaders randomly?"

"Since you have imagined so much, you can imagine answers to these questions as well." The bitch was not ready to supply any clues. She was assessing how much I knew.

"Karnataka Assembly Elections were held in May. Someone or some organisation abroad wanted to influence the elections, and, more specifically, support candidates from a minority Sunni community. Elections in south India are a costly affair. So Anbu wanted to move a large amount of cash from offshore accounts to selected political candidates in the first week of April.

"He was getting money through the Hawala route on a regular basis. But the money he got was not huge. This time it was huge, since it was meant to fund election expenses.

"Only few people in the company knew about the Hawala transactions. I am guessing the Tamil ogres who beat me up in Globosoft office last week are the ones who knew. One of them hatched a plan. He introduced Swati Gupta into the equation. Swati slept with Anbu and became privy to his secrets. She vanished with the money that came on 7 April."

"So, what is your problem?" Roopa asked. "Why are you poking your nose in our matter?"

"My concern is finding Swati."

"Then find her. Why concern us?"

"Why are you people so perturbed?" I asked.

"Have you ever managed a business? You do what you have to do to run a business. Which multinational corporation in this world survives without hiding some money in tax havens?"

"Yours is a software company. Why do you pay kickbacks?"

"Who are you to ask questions? Who are you to judge us? We run a business. We do what we have to do to stay in business."

After a pause, she asked: "How much for the diary?"

"I did not imply that I need money for the diary."

"But we want to pay. We will keep it professional. We will take the diary and sign a non-disclosure agreement with you. You agree not to disclose anything you learnt about the company. In return, we will transfer fees to your bank account. It will be a full white transaction. No Hawala, no cash."

"Attractive proposition! I can consider it once my case is closed. For now, this diary is part of the investigation I conducted on Bhide's expenses for finding his wife. I cannot violate my commitments to Bhide."

"How will this diary help Bhide get his wife back?" she asked, getting irritated.

"I don't know. I don't know much about what's happening around. Your goons are not ready to come clean on what happened. You also choose to stay silent. So it remains with me as leverage, till I understand what's going on. It is unethical of me to let go of a leverage that will help Bhide's case."

"Oh come on. Ethics do not sound good when coming out of your mouth. I know what you did at Pharmabus. I did my homework." She had touched a raw nerve. I pushed her and wriggled out of her embrace.

"You know nothing about what happened at Pharmabus. My moral issues are mine. They are not subject to your comments and criticism. Now get lost."

I opened the door and held it for her.

"Sorry if I have insulted you in any way. You know how difficult it is to do business in India. I have partnered with people and grown over the years. I have turned every threat into an opportunity. I would love to partner with you, on your terms. Till then, hold on to my secrets," Roopa said in a reconciliatory tone, and left.

Was this the demoness Sneha had warned me about?

15

Kediaji

Sixty-year-old Ramakrishna Kedia (also called Kediaji) is a portly man, overflowing on all sides of his torso due to his weakness for cow ghee. He is five feet and eight inches tall. A missing tooth in his upper jaw gives him a comical look whenever he laughs. Kediaji offered his prayers to goddess Lakshmi and started work for the day. As a habit, Kediaji takes his cash balance at the end of the day home, and brings it back in the morning. This day, he opened a suitcase, counted the cash, and put it in a drawer in his office table.

His routine starts with a review of the accounts. He maintained a 'single entry' accounting system, in the traditional Marwari fashion. He matched the entries and cross-checked the balance with cash-in-hand. The cash position at the end of the previous day was Rs. 1.20 crores – a surprising figure, going by the looks of his run-down shop. He stayed in a luxurious penthouse in Bandra, which he has renovated many times in the last twenty years. But the shop has been as it is. Of course, Kediaji repaired the shop when it became necessary, but nothing more than what was necessary. He liked it this way.

For a shop where he transacted in lakhs, often crores of rupees daily, maintaining a low profile was a necessity. He had no fear of thieves and dacoits. He paid off the local strongman, and was on good terms with the area's police chowki. His mortal enemies were sleuths from the tax department, who could put his business in a limbo. He was once raided in early 2000s, after the department found mention of his name in the tally accounts of a stupid client. The client had mentioned in narration to some cash entries that the money was paid by Kediaji.

It took Kediaji years to recoup the damage from the raid and move ahead. The department had then seized his accounts and used them to target his other clients. It branded him a *Hawala agent* and shamed him in open court proceedings. The department officers treated every transaction they found in his accounts as income, and imposed taxes and penalties that were many times more than his actual income.

Not content with the damage, the department had referred his case to the Enforcement Directorate and the Economic Offence Wing for criminal proceedings. Luckily for him, the standards of bringing criminal charges are more rigorous than charging anyone for tax evasion. He managed to wriggle out in a few years, but after suffering substantial pain and agony.

A business like his is always vulnerable to income tax action. To minimise the damage, Kediaji maintained accounts only for thirty days in his office. Older accounts were packed in red cloth and stored in an attic in his brother-in-law's house. He regularly deleted his mobile communication with clients.

There was a massive income tax action on seven Hawaladars in the area a year back, in which taxmen used computer forensic experts to retrieve deleted whatsApp and SMS messages. This put him under greater strain. He started changing his mobile phone every month. After sometime, the arduous work of transferring the address list from one phone to another overwhelmed him. He hasn't changed his phone in six months.

Kediaji's office boy appeared an hour later, and made tea for him. The boy doubled up as his cash handler, and went about collecting cash from clients who had to remit their money abroad. For overseas customers who wanted to send money to their near ones in Mumbai, Kediaji offered a facility for home delivery of cash. The single office boy handled both doorstep collection and doorstep delivery.

Quite unexpectedly, a tall man, about six feet and two inches in height, entered his office. Dressed in jeans and a white shirt, he had a goatee and long hair that he had tied into a ponytail. He sat down across from Kediaji and asked in chaste Hindi, "Are you Ramakrishna Kedia?"

He was too bossy for Kediaji's tastes. "Yes, what do you want?"

"I want you to answer a few questions."

"What about? Who are you?"

"My name is Bakshi. I have been hired by Globosoft United States to solve a mystery for them. Ever heard of the company?"

"Selvam's company?" Kediaji whispered.

"Anbu Selvam is just an employee in the company. The owners are based in America. Surely you know that."

"Well, yes… no… I am only concerned where my services are called for. My partner in Dubai also knows nothing."

So the money had come from Dubai through the Hawala route, Saby Biswas noted – for that's who Bakshi really was. He was here on Digyen Burmah's request to extract information from Kedia.

"Well, no one told me anything. Anbu, Palani or Shashi."

"My appointment is beyond their pay grade," Saby Biswas said. This is the point when Kediaji would call Palani for confirmation. Biswas had to scuttle that and overwhelm Kediaji.

"I have been investigating a fraud involving you for a month now. Roopalaxmi Sivanarayanan has been cooperating with me. I have concluded that these Tamil brats who work in the local Globosoft office have not pulled off the fraud. That leaves only one man who knew about the cash movement – *you!* Where is the cash?"

"Are you mad? No! Where is Anbu? How about, we sit with Anbu and—"

"We are in this situation because of Anbu. It was because of his lack of control. That's why all this has happened in the first place. We will play at a different level now. Peep out of your balcony," Saby said.

Kediaji reluctantly looked around. It was broad daylight, and the portico was bustling with customers. His neighbours would come running if he cried out to them. The local boys he patronised would then arrive in less than ten minutes. This assured him.

He went to the back window and peeped out. Two Innova cars were parked at a distance, facing away from him. 'Investigation

Wing' and 'Income Tax Department' were written in bold red letters on the bonnet of both the vehicles.

Kediaji's throat dried as he tried to gulp his saliva. He rushed off to the portico and looked at the road in front of his complex. An Innova car was parked at a distance. Parking an Innova car on a busy and narrow road is an anomaly he did not miss.

"What is this?" Kediaji bellowed on coming back into his shop.

"My clients in the States think that someone has to pay for what happened. You need to know that there are consequences."

"But it's not my fault that the girl cheated Anbu.' He said, out of fear.

'Since when have you known the girl?" Saby asked.

"I don't know her. I have never met her before she picked up the cash, or have ever met her after that day."

"Where is the cash?"

"How do I know? I gave it to her."

"You do not sound convincing," Saby said. "I had strict instructions to give a complaint in writing to the Department that you are running a fraud Hawala racket. That's why I have pulled the sleuths along. I am yet to signal them which shop they need to raid. You still have a chance to come clean."

"I swear by goddess Lakshmi, I have no role in the fraud. Someone delivered cash to my partner in Dubai and gave him the code. My partner sent me the code. I was supposed to deliver the cash to anyone who gives me the ten rupee note from which the code was taken. Since the amount was huge, I had to arrange for transfer through other Hawaladars. Once the money was ready, I called Anbu and informed him. He rarely comes; he sends someone with the note.

"The woman produced the ten rupee note. The serial number matched with the code my partner sent me. So I gave her the cash," Kediaji explained, anxious not to be misunderstood. "The woman was nervous that day," Kediaji continued when Saby did not react. "She was taking the bags without even counting and I pointed that out. I phoned Anbu to inform him that I had delivered the cash, but he did not pick up. She was here for so long to count cash, but Anbu did not call back. What could I have done? She had the code. I had to give her the cash."

"How long was she here with you?"

"More than half an hour."

"Why did she take so long to count the notes?" Saby asked.

"She would have taken an eternity to count the notes. She just counted the bundles. That too, she was not interested. I insisted, because earlier too clients have taken cash and then told me that the money was short. Like I told you earlier too, she counted on my insistence."

"Why will it take her half an hour only to count bundles?"

"You make the calculation *maalik.* Forty crores in bundles of hundred. 2000 rupees notes… comes to two thousand bundles. I had packed them into eight big bags. She had to count two fifty bundles in each bag and put them back. We are lucky that we are living in post-demonetisation time. Pink notes take one third of the space that thousand rupees bundles took. Else she would have had to carry twenty-five bags."

Saby was taken aback. Forty crores in a single transfer? Where did these guys get this kind of money? It might be politically active people's money, managed by Globosoft's promoters.

"How did she take the bags?"

"In the uber cab she had brought, a big SUV. I have told this to Palani too. Again, I did not care to note the make or vehicle number. That's not my job."

Saby dramatically shook his head and exclaimed. "Have I made a mistake by bringing in the income tax wallas?"

"Yes, yes. I earned my commission, an honest man's commission."

From a dishonest activity, Saby thought to himself.

"You can tell them that you were mistaken… that I am only an LIC agent," Kediaji said.

The stranger got up and left his shop. Kediaji crept outside and peeped at the stranger. He heaved a sigh of relief when the stranger left the complex.

Saby Biswas had staged a small heist of his own to get information from Kediaji. Hawaladars operate by a strict code of secrecy, and will not give out information in any normal condition. So he had to use the one thing every Hawaladar fears – the Department. He got three cars from the Pharmabus office and placed Income Tax Department's name boards on them. That did the trick.

16

An Unexpected Twist

How much does a person need to live a decent life? How much does one need to live an extravagant life? A crore? Two crores? Ten? How much excess you are left with, if you have forty crores in hand? The interest that this money earns is enough to live a life of extravagance.

And now, Swati Gupta had this money. Or if she is dead, the Tourist!

The very magnitude of this heist dawned on me after Biswas da told me what he learnt from the Hawaladar. The plan was flawless. The Tourist did meticulous research, worked patiently for over two years and ran a con that did not involve a single bullet fire. He looted black money, something that cannot be reported to the police. He hid himself behind layers. Even after frantically searching for three months, Roopa and her men have not managed to identify him.

As for the source, it could very well be kickback paid in an offshore account, as Biswas da believed. It might have been brought into India to fund the elections. Or to run a campaign for some lobby group.

The forty crores would have definitely gone to fund elections. It could not be mere coincidence that the money was moved just before Karnataka elections. As per the diary entries, regular payments were made to clerics and local politicians in Western Karnataka and North Kerala, and there was no seeming connection between them. The clerics and politicians were influential in local Sunni Muslim communities, but they did not belong to any single group or organisation.

I was puzzling over these facts when I got a call from Mallya. Apparently Bopanna had reached out to him to reach out to me.

"Digyen bro! You are fishing in deep waters," Mallya said. "Bopanna phoned. He wants a deal with you. It seems you have something that belongs to him. He is making a generous offer. Offered me ten percent for brokering the deal."

"Did he tell you what is in my possession that belongs to him?" I asked.

"He was cryptic. I was hoping you will tell me."

"What's the offer?"

"Twenty lakhs."

"Ten percent is yours. Sounds small by your standards."

"Not at all. Two lakhs is a good commission for me. I will stand guarantee for you and facilitate the deal. Why should I expect the sky for it?"

"But how do you know it's generous? What if he wants me to give him a diamond worth five crores by paying twenty lakhs? You should have found out what he wants from me, and how valuable it is to him. Or else, how do you cut a deal?"

"Okay. Seems you are not in the mood for a deal. Will let him know."

"But thank you. He was trying to put his weight around… became a puppy after hearing your name," I said.

"That's true, bro. He is shit scared of me. I found a way to stay close to the commissioner. That's why."

"I forwarded your number to the party looking for land approval in the industrial area development board. Did anyone get in touch with you?" I asked.

"Yes bro. I think I will seal that deal."

"Cool," I said and disconnected.

The thing about hyenas is that they punctually arrive to partake in the spoils. Mallya had no idea what this was all about. I doubt Bopanna knows much. But they have smelt money, and are now salivating for a share.

I reviewed the clues I had collected till now. I dozed off while still studying the clues. I woke up when my smartphone rang. It was Nidhi.

"Digyen, you are in trouble," Nidhi said. She was breathing frantically. "You were right about Palani Kumar."

"How do you know? Relax! Are you alright? Where are you?" I asked.

"I am going to Bhide's home. Palani Kumar has committed suicide, and has mentioned you in his suicide note."

"What the fuck? Why me? I don't even know that guy. Is this a joke? I am keeping…"

"He has mentioned in his suicide note that he and Swati were lovers. They had met in Kathmandu and fallen in love. Together, they had planned to cheat Anbu Selvam and elope. Swati double-crossed him and vanished."

"So I was correct," I said.

"Yes. But that is not why Palani committed suicide. He has said that you came and threatened him. You got call records of his phone conversations and blackmailed him that you will expose him."

"Blackmail?" I asked.

"Did you do it, Digyen?"

"No... not at all. I told him that I suspected him. I had seen his phone records, which showed frequent chats and calls to Swati. I threatened him that I would expose him, yes, but I did not blackmail him. Blackmail is a strong word to use."

"I don't know if he has used that word. We will know when we see the suicide note. In the note, he blames you for putting him under immense mental pressure. It means..."

"It means I can be charged with abetment of suicide," I completed her. But I have a witness. I have never spoken with Palani alone. Puwaiya was with me that day. But he was drunk. And he may be having a criminal record. Shit! Let's meet at Bhide's place and assess the damage."

▼

Bhide stayed in a low-cost housing complex on Banerghatta Road, close to IIM campus.

I arrived at his flat with Puwaiya to find Nidhi consoling him. He lived in a sparse house that was not whitewashed for a long time now. The paint was peeling on all walls; paint on the drawing-room walls was mixed with soot and dust. The money he was spending to find his wife was significant, considering the condition he lived in. I resolved to make him pay my fees even if he bled through his nose.

Bhide was inconsolable. A man had committed suicide, but all he was worried about was Swati.

My Swati, why did you do it Swati, I loved you Swati. I will not forgive you Swati, blah blah.

His attitude did not help me. I was mired in guilt. Palani did not appear to be a pussy. I would have handled him differently had I known that he was a chicken-hearted person. But then, you never know what snaps in the mind of a man with suicidal tendencies.

The ever resourceful Puwaiya offered me a joint. He said it would make me feel better. I don't usually do drugs, but did not mind a puff or two , hoping to feel comforted. After all, there was also the matter of my name in the suicide note. Police can construe it in any way. I am not a registered investigator. No one has reported any crime to the police. To any third party, my confronting Palani will appear like my interference in his personal life. I would be the logical reason forcing him to suicide.

Information on the suicide seeped in from Bhide's colleagues in bits and pieces.

This is what apparently happened. Palani's maid reached his house at eight in the morning. He opened the door for her, and paid her the entire month's salary. He asked her to take all vegetables in the fridge with her, as he did not need them anymore. He locked his bedroom from inside.

Palani did not respond when the maid called him out for breakfast. She banged at the door, but still there was no response. The maid finally called the security guard, who called the building maintenance boys. They broke open the room to find Palani hanging from the ceiling.

Palani had written a long note in Tamil, which the police confirmed was in his handwriting. He was not as unkind to me as Nidhi initially made it out to be. Palani mentioned in the note that he was an orphan. His upbringing was supported by Roopalaxmi's father, due to which he was deeply obliged to her and Anbu. But he was a compulsive gambler, and was knee deep in debts. He recruited Preeti from Kathmandu and brought her to Mumbai to win Anbu's confidence and loot him.

Their plan was to go to Malaysia together after robbing Anbu. But she double-crossed him and fled. Palani was left with his guilt and pain at being deceived. The final push came when Bhide hired me to find his wife. I got his phone records and threatened to expose him if he did not tell where Preeti was. The guilt of being exposed to Anbu overwhelmed him, and he decided to end his life.

If the translation was correct and communicated correctly through Chinese whispers to Bhide's colleagues to him to me, then I was safe from abetment charges.

A poor man was dead. That's unfortunate. But I had nothing to do with it. I had confronted him with evidence. Palani has mentioned the same in his suicide note. I will be asked about where I got his phone records. I can always say that I got clues from an anonymous informer and did not actually possess the phone records. I regained my composure and cheerful spirits. I even went on to console Bhide and impart words of wisdom to him.

"But I… I cannot find someone like Swati. I still find it hard to believe," Bhide said between his cries. Puwaiya's joint was of a fine quality; it was already giving me a gratifying high. I recalled that Bidhya had asked me to communicate her concerns about Swati's family to Bhide.

"Bhide, you have to be strong. You have responsibilities. Swati's real name is Preeti, as Nidhi must have already told you. She has an ailing father and four kids in Kathmandu. They are in dire condition since Swati no longer sends them money. They survived on Swati's income. Now they are your responsibility. You have to take care of them."

"Why will I take care of them? She is a cheater! She cheated and lied. Let her take care of her family," Bhide said as his face convoluted with anger and frustration.

"Arre baba. She cannot take care of the family. She is on the run from your MD and his goons. How do you expect the poor girl to take care of her family," I said. Bhide fumed at Swati for leaving her family to his care, without realising the derision in my advice.

Nidhi did not find my humour amusing and shooed me away (although she had a hard time controlling her giggles).

"Best way you can help Bhide now is to leave from here," Nidhi said. "He is stressed. I think only his therapist can help him in this condition."

"Good idea," I said. "Let's call his therapist."

"I tried to call. The number Bhide gave me is not reachable. I can't find another number on the web," Nidhi added.

"Then give me the address. I will go to his clinic and take his advice."

Nidhi gave me an address for Bhide's therapist. I promised to reach out to the therapist and left Bhide's house.

▼

I was still stoned. It made absolutely no sense to waste the high in searching for Bhide's therapist. Puwaiya and I hit a military hotel. We cheered to the memory of Palani Kumar and gulped glasses of Old Monk.

I got a whatsApp message from an unknown number, asking me how I am. I clicked on the display picture and saw an uber-stylish picture of Roopalaxmi.

RL: How are you?

Me: Pulling around. How are you?

RL: I am in shock... Palani was family.

Me: I understand.

RL: In shock... but not in mourning.

RL: He betrayed me.

Me: Seriously?

Me: Give him a break... he killed himself out of guilt.

RL: He killed himself because the woman betrayed him the same way he betrayed me.

RL: I am going back to US on Sunday.

Me: Okay... Time for me to head back to Mumbai.

Me: Guess we will not get to know each other better.

RL: I want to know you better. :)

RL: We are so similar... rational, smart and intelligent.

RL: Anbu has released a press note... that a female employee stole software codes from the company.

RL: We have not pressed charges bcuz the codes are 4 an earlier version... now outdated.

Me: Whereas she slipped away with 40C.
Me: Where did you get the figure?
RL: Never mind – You still have something that belongs to me.
RL: Name your price.
Me: I am getting paid for my time here.
Me: I will hand over your diary tomorrow.
RL: I will come with a handsome reward.
Me: Keep your reward. I don't cut deals on shady acts.
RL: You are a complex man, Digyen Burmah!
RL: I will be at your hotel tomorrow morning.

I had wrestled with the idea of taking her offer. On one level, it was fine arbitrage. But, on another, it just sounded immoral.

Puwaiya shook me out of my reverie by talking about Palani. He was slightly emotional that the good man who had offered him foreign liquor in a posh hotel killed himself. He moaned about why all good people die early.

For me, it was an occasion to celebrate. I should not take any credit, but I was on the right path. I would have solved the case eventually. I patted myself and smirked.

But was the case really solved?

17

The Turning Point

I woke up at nine on Saturday morning to find Puwaiya sleeping expansively on the bed, a leg resting on me. His mouth was open and he was snoring noisily.

I went to the washroom and washed my face. There was a hangover lingering from the earlier night that was bothering me. I could not remember what it was. It was not the *Old Monk*. The Monk never tortures its followers. It was an idea that occurred to me while I was drinking.

Puwaiya and I were chit-chatting in the Military Hotel, when he said something important. Both of us were heavily drunk by then. His input struck me like lightning… but soon eased out of my mind under the influence of Old Monk.

I went into the bedroom and tried to wake Puwaiya. I asked him about the important news he had given me the previous night. He was completely blank. I asked him if he had shared with me a new angle or a new fact about Bhide's case. He was blank. The inept fellow did not even remember where he was last night, and what he was doing in my hotel room.

I got a call from Nidhi. I needed privacy to speak with her, so I sent Puwaiya to the washroom, closed the washroom door, and took Nidhi's call.

"Hey… good morning."

"Good morning Digyen. Where did you go last night? I phoned you four times in the night, no reply."

"I was wasted. What's the matter?"

"Just wanted to meet you. I left Bhide's place late… at quarter past eight."

"How is he doing?"

"He is hurt. Did you get an appointment with his therapist? Don't tell me that you did not go to the therapist's place?"

"Ah, I had gone… but, it was closed," I lied. "The guard asked me to come back today. I will fix a meeting today itself."

After a brief pause, she said, "Okay! How are you?"

"Puzzled!"

"What do you mean?"

"Something does not add up. This Puwaiya told me something last night that made me wonder if we have really solved the case."

"But Palani confessed in his suicide note."

"I know. Something is off. I just don't recall what Puwaiya told me last night."

"Ask him."

"That worthless fellow does not remember a thing. He was neck deep in rum last night. I had to drag him out of the bar. He had passed out."

After our conversation, we decided to meet for breakfast the next morning. I looked at my smartphone's internet browser after I disconnected. I had last searched for 'Indoctrination + Wahhabism + India'.

The internet search keywords provided a cue to me about the important discussion I had with Puwaiya the night before. Puwaiya had become emotional about Palani and said that the fellow must have suffered tremendous personal suffering, having been deserted as an infant. The kind Imam in Palakkad who adopted him gave him a father's love, but he never got a mother's love. I corrected him, saying that Palani was probably a Tamil Hindu.

"Palani spoke classical Tamil when we first met in the hotel's lobby," I recalled Puwaiya saying. "But started speaking a different dialect of Tamil with many words from Malayalam once we became informal at the bar. It was Palakkad Tamil, a dialect spoken in Palakkad district of Kerala. I know because I have relatives down there. Palani confirmed that he is from Palakkad. In fact, he studied in a hundred-year-old seminary started by Chalilakath Kunahmed Haji."

These were Puwaiya's last words last night, before he passed out. I had googled about this reformer Chalilakath Haji and found that he was a Sunni scholar and revered among Malabar Muslims as an educational reformer during British rule in India. When the British introduced a colonial education system in India, there was stiff resistance from many conservative leaders. The Muslim *ulama* had issued anti-British *fatwas* denouncing the new education system. Chalilakath Haji is credited with fighting the conservatives in his community and introducing reforms through the so-called Madrasa movement. He introduced Malayalam grammar in madrasas (where Arabic is primary means of pedagogy), encouraged students to engage in different streams of education, and established libraries within madrasas.

The point is, if Palani was brought up within the madrasa education system, Palani Kumar was definitely an alias and not a real name. Someone educated in a madrasa would generally have a Mohammedan name. Why use an alias? This brings me back to the affairs at Globosoft. If it is not a real business but a front, what is the real nature of its business?

I went back to my phone internet browser to see what the keywords 'indoctrination + Wahhabism + India' returned. The first search result was a news report of 2011 alleging Saudi charities for radicalising the youth in Kashmir valley by pumping huge funds through the Hawala channel.

There is a popular theory about radicalisation of the youth in Kashmir valley, which the report alluded to. Wahhabism is a fundamentalist ideology based on an austere and puritanical interpretation of the Islam faith. This ideology evolved out of the beliefs of a Saudi cleric by the name of Muhammad ibn Abd-al-Wahhab who lived in the eighteenth century. Abd-al-Wahhab had developed an alliance with the House of Saud, which went on to become the ruling dynasty of Arabia. To this day, Saud rulers remain devoted to Wahhabism and the Kingdom of Saudi Arabia sets aside a chunk of income they earn from oil for spreading Wahhabism. *Dawah Wahhabiyya* is a mission to spread Wahhabi ideas around the world. Charities backed by the kingdom and its princes spend billions of dollars every year on mosques, schools, free books and scholarships, in order to promote Wahhabism.

The theory goes that some of the funds raised by proponents of Wahhabism are pumped into mosques and madrasas in Kashmir, and used to radicalise the youth in Kashmir. Kashmiris are being weaned away from the tolerant and secular Sufi traditions by these mosques and madrasas run with Saudi money. Elsewhere in the world, funds collected in the name of spreading Wahhabism have been used to patronise jehad and cause communal tensions.

In Indonesia, for example, Java island is known for the peaceful coexistence of Muslims, Christians and Buddhists, and common cultural practices can be found in rituals of different religious communities. But scholars educated in schools teaching Wahhabism asserted Islamic primacy among faiths, and adopted more orthodox practices. Hardline Sunni Muslims in Indonesia have vandalised Buddhist temples and Christian Churches, and attacked members of Ahmaddiya and Shia sects.

Palani Kumar had taken offence when I accused him of swindling Selvam's money, and had said that he only cared about the cause, not money. When I asked him about the cause, he evaded the question.

Selvam rotated large amount of money in offshore accounts and sent them from Dubai to India through the Hawala route. Since Wahhabi charitable trusts have been linked to some international terrorist organisations, the Financial Action Task Force (FATF) can freeze bank accounts linked to Wahhabism in any jurisdiction. Its financing routes can be choked overnight.

That's why the diary was so important to Roopalaxmi and Selvam. It contained description of money trail from bank accounts in tax havens all the way to Sunni clerics and sectarian leaders in south India. Further analysis of the source may reveal many people working in shadows to influence elections or fuelling communal strife in India.

▼

Puwaiya's state of bliss was disturbed by an upset stomach. He woke up and found himself in a spic and span washroom. He lifted the commode bowl's lid and relieved himself. He pressed the tank button to flush, but no water came out. He was actually pressing a sticker, but nevertheless blamed the commode for malfunctioning. Taking things into his hands, he lifted the lid off the commode tank and looked inside.

A packet carefully wrapped in plastic was stuck to the tanks' inside. He took it out and reset the tank's lid. Then he again pressed the sticker, mistaking it for the button. It did not work.

He put the lid back to cover the bowl and hoped that his boss wouldn't smell his filth in the commode.

Puwaiya sipped on his moonshine and tore the plastic off the packet. The packet contained a diary and some papers. He laughed at whoever put papers in a commode tank, and went back into his meditative stage.

▼

I was lost in my thoughts when I heard the doorbell ring. This was the time housekeeping personnel came daily. I opened the door to refuse the service, but was taken aback to find Roopalaxmi standing there.

"What are you doing here?"

"As we had agreed yesterday… did you forget?"

It came back to me. I had messaged her that I would hand over the diary to her in the morning today.

"And since I was in a cheerful mood, I brought you some cake," Roopalaxmi said and barged in.

"But… but I don't have it yet," I resisted. "How about I get it and we meet later in the evening?"

"I have no other work. I can give you company for the entire time," she said as she inched more and more inside my room.

"But I have other things to do. I have to wrap up my work before leaving," I resisted. By now, she had seated herself at my study table.

"Why are you acting so nervous? Like a teenage lover?" Roopalaxmi asked and eased her legs on my bed. She was wearing a white top and pink shorts. "Who knows, if you play smart, you may get a piece of Roopa today! I am in an unusually generous mood."

I thought it would be better to humour her and take her out of the room. I could lose her somewhere outside and get back to the hotel to secure the diary.

"This ACP Bopanna guy was getting on my nerves. So I kept the diary at a friend's house in Lavelle Road," I lied. "I have lunch with him. I was planning to get it after lunch."

"Where is it? I can send someone to fetch it," Roopalaxmi said.

"Better you come with me to Lavelle Road. That way I will get more time to savour the beauty called Roopa," I said and offered her tea. She agreed to a cup of masala tea.

I prepared tea for her, while realising that a key actor in what could be a terror financing ring was sitting in my room.

There is no way I am going to hand over the diary to her. Black money is one thing and terror financing is another. A company transferring black money is, no doubt, on the wrong side of law. But it's a norm for companies to engage in such transgressions. It is stealing from the government. I am no one to judge them, especially when I have no official liability to report them. But financing of extremism is different. It's organised crime, and probably the severest. I have a responsibility as a citizen to report it to the authorities.

I poured the tea in a cup and turned to give it to Roopalaxmi, just to find that she was looking into my laptop.

"Why are you looking for Islamic fundamentalism in Malabar?" she asked. "And you have been searching for Mujahideen sleeper cells in Karnataka." Roopalaxmi looked miffed and angry.

I shrugged and said, "Just curious"

Roopalaxmi stared at me intently, with a bit of disappointment.

"Yasin Bhatkal. You know Yasin Bhatkal, the Indian Mujahideen leader? He was from Bhatkal on the coast in western Karnataka. And Nazir Dabede, another Indian Mujahideen operative, was from the coastal area in Kerala. They had set up a training camp for terrorists in Coorg, disguised it as a farm for ginger cultivation," I said.

"So?"

"So I got curious about these terrorists, and googled about them," I said. I could see Roopalaxmi was not convinced.

"Anbu!" Roopalaxmi called out. The shorty Anbu Selvam barged into the room along with Shashi Selvam and two others who had beaten me in Globosoft office. I could identify one of them as Bala. Bala closed the door behind him.

"I knew something was off when you refused to take my offer for money. A duplicitous man like you will not give away something we so desperately want back, so easily. So I brought back up," Roopalaxmi said and took out a 9 mm handgun from her purse. Her men had also come armed.

"For the record, I did not know that you guys are launderers or illicit financiers last night, when I promised to give back the diary to you. Maybe you have judged me all wrong," I said and tried to put on a charm offensive.

"Raise your hands bastard, or I will shoot at your groins," Roopalaxmi said. I meekly complied. There was nothing to be done, no way out. I was surrounded by members of some notorious terror financing ring, who were fighting for survival, in a hotel room.

"Check for the diary in his belongings," Roopalaxmi told Bala. Bala nodded and started rummaging through my personal belongings.

"You think you are some saint for taking kickbacks and betraying your employer? And we, who risk our lives for the cause, are terrorists?" Anbu Selvam said.

"I never took any kickback. Pharmabus was disposing expired medicines in black markets. I informed its competitors, so that they could blow the whistle. I did not take a single pie," I said. I had not tried to explain myself to friends and family, who came up with this jibe. I did not understand why I felt a burning need to defend myself to these felons.

"Whaat makes you think that we are terrarist?" Shashi asked in his heavy accent, as he peeped into my laptop.

"Please note, I did not directly call you terrorists. But you bring money into India without Home Ministry approval, violate FCRA law, and use it to radicalise people and fund election expenses in India. That's as good as engaging in extremism. Forty crores in a single transfer is too big for the Hawala route. Till 2014, you brought more than hundred crores into India through a Trust. The Trust was blocked in 2015, and so you brought in money through the Hawala route. But why are you desperate to bring money into India and distribute it among clerics? Because they are sympathetic to your cause… because they provide you asylum and turn a blind eye to your activities. You try to radicalise poor believers into believing your ideology of hatred and intolerance.

"Your company is a front. I should have realised that when I first analysed your company's accounts. It takes overseas contracts and, in turn, subcontracts it to a couple of domestic software companies. You don't do any work by yourself. You have not made any profit since you started operations. You do not have any valuable IP of your own. The company is a pass-through entity. It has entered into an arrangement with the domestic software companies by which their receipts pass through your accounts. This way, Globosoft can show high turnover. It gives you prestige and access to people in high positions… a cover to lobby for your cause and freedom to move around in the garb of corporate managers."

"And you think our cause is bad?" Roopalaxmi asked.

"I don't have any thoughts for your cause. I just don't want to get involved with terrorists. That's why, I keep my peace, and you keep your peace. I can get the diary from my friend and give it to you. Then you go your way, I go my way. What say you?"

"Not after you have known so much. We cannot take the chance," Roopalaxmi said, with a grimace that looked like real concern for me. "You just can't keep your nose where it is... you have to poke it everywhere. We had to sacrifice Palani just so that we stop you on your tracks. But no, you had to keep digging."

"You killed Palani, right?"

"No, he killed himself! To put an end to your investigation... God bless him."

"He committed suicide to create a smokescreen? So that I would think that the case was solved?"

"Yes. He told us that you suspected him of being Swati's partner. He thought that the best way to stop you on your trail is to close the case for you. There would be too much spotlight on us if we killed you. So he offered to commit suicide, to stop the matter from escalating," Anbu Selvam said. He was in tears.

"Blowing your head will be our tribute to his memory." A mean ogre standing behind Anbu said. I recalled how ruthlessly he had kicked me in the stomach in Globosoft office. I was already sweating. This could be my last day.

"We sacrificed one of our own rather than kill you because we don't have any enmity with you. We bring this money to do charity and help poor Muslim brothers and sisters," Roopalaxmi said.

"You sacrificed him because you were afraid that you will be exposed if I kept digging," I said. "Now relax and think. The problem still remains for you. You have been captured in the

CCTV cameras of this hotel. If you kill me in my room, the police will dig deep, and you will still be exposed."

"We have no other option at this stage. We will try to manage the police, and lay low till this blows over," Anbu said.

"It's not that simple. I am a specialist in fraud detection. All my friends work in this field. They will keep digging your muck even if you manage the police. Look, we need to think about it like adults," I proposed.

Roopalaxmi sniggered and told her men. "I don't have patience for this. Anbu, shoot yourself!"

"As you say Lokka," Anbu said reverentially. He touched the muzzle of his gun on his forehead and pulled the trigger. Blood from his brain splattered on my shirt.

Roopalaxmi looked nonchalantly and ordered her fourth goon to remove Anbu's fingerprints from his gun.

All of this happened so fast that I could not cope with it. My immediate response was of numbness.

When I regained my composure, I saw Anbu Selvam lying lifeless beside me. I went on my knees and crawled to Roopalaxmi and cried for mercy. I was ready to join the ISIS – or Hezbollah or Al Qaeda – if she salvaged my life. I was ready to be her slave for life if she showed me mercy.

Roopalaxmi pointed her 9mm at me and said, "Anbu Selvam came here with his brother, because you were blackmailing him that you will expose his relationship with Swati Gupta. You had earlier blackmailed Palani. Palani committed suicide under duress. Anbu turned up without any money and threatened to hand you over to the police. You killed Anbu in the tussle that ensued. Shashi took out his gun and shot at you – in self-defence. Other two are witnesses… personal staff escorting Anbu."

The bitch now looked like a Chandi. I swore to take my wife's intuitions seriously if I escaped this situation alive.

"Does the story sound convincing to you? Or do you think police will keep digging-aa?" Shashi said from behind my back. I looked around and found him pointing his gun at me.

▼

Puwaiya woke up with a start on hearing what appeared to be a gunshot. He found himself in a spic and span washroom.

Who the fuck fired that gun?

He soon recalled that he was in his boss' hotel room. His boss was still in the room, while he was in a washroom. He took out his gun and took up the posture of Don Mutthapa Rai's gunslinger behind the washroom door. He put his ear to the door and counted a woman and three male voices other than his boss. He heard his boss snivel pathetically.

Soon, his eyes fell on his moonshine bottle lying on the washroom dresser. The quarter bottle still had some moonshine left. He put the moonshine in his left pocket and complimentary toiletries in his right pocket. He tucked the diary and toilet papers inside his vest.

Assuming that the woman also carried a gun, it would be very difficult for Puwaiya to overwhelm them all by himself. He would open the door and disarm the first in sight. Then he would dive down and fix his target on the second. He would shoot and disarm the second.

By that time, the third and fourth will be pointing their guns on him. He could take on only one of them. If he tackles the third, the fourth would shoot him. He hoped that the fourth would shoot him in the stomach, where the diary and toilet papers would abate the bullet's impact.

▼

The best way of handling a near-death situation is to keep calm and think. That was one thing I was unable to do when facing the muzzle of Shashi Selvam's gun.

The image of Anbu Selvam merrily blowing his brains out struck me like a scene from a horror movie. It shook something inside me, and I regressed to a more innocent past.

I turned back to Roopalaxmi and got hold of her legs. I begged her to leave me. Bala could not find the diary after searching through my belongings and the room's fixtures, and turned towards the washroom.

And then a miracle happened!

As Bala opened the washroom door, Puwaiya came out in a squatting posture. Putting a leg forward, he shot at Bala's groins. His shot wound Bala and he fell down with a moan. Shashi, standing to the right of the washroom door, swerved reflexively and shot at Puwaiya. But Puwaiya was ready for it. He dived to the right and aimed at Shashi's hand.

Puwaiya's hit was a very difficult one, if you think about it. He was not aiming at Shashi's body, lest the bastard die. He was aiming at his hand, in order to incapacitate him. He dived, quickly composed himself, and shot at the hand. And he hit the target.

Roopalaxmi's fourth gunman was busy polishing Anbu's gun. They were planning to put my fingerprints on it after shooting me, so that I could be implicated for Anbu's death. He was taken by surprise. He aimed Anbu's gun at Puwaiya. Simultaneously, Roopalaxmi aimed her cute 9mm at Puwaiya. I was crying between her legs. I saw an opening there, to save the day. I don't mean in the context of Roopalaxmi's legs, but in the given situation.

I jumped on Roopalaxmi. Placing my left hand on her fulsome breast for support, I used my right hand to move her gun hand when she was about to pull the trigger. Her shot landed on her last standing gunman. Then, I twisted her arm, making her drop the gun. Puwaiya asked me to hurry out of the room. He had opened the door. Appreciating her for the firm bosoms, I dashed out of the room.

Few neighbours were peeping out of their rooms. Few security personnel had reached the floor. We rushed past the security personnel as Roopalaxmi came out of the room. She shouted slurs at me and shot her 9mm blindly. We were rushing down the fire exit stairs by then.

I recalled after alighting a few steps that I had left the diary in the washroom and asked Puwaiya to stop.

"I have to go back to the room. There is a diary… an important diary that I cannot leave there. That's evidence that these people engage in illicit finance and I don't have a copy. It has important bank account details," I explained to Puwaiya.

"Why worry about a diary, sir? Life is most important. You can get other diaries from market. Diary no use… see, I using diary and toilet paper as vest to protect from bullets," Puwaiya said.

'What diary?'

"Some idiot had put diary inside the commode. The commode water was not working. It still has my filth sir."

18

Blurred Boundaries

Three Months Later

October is an unusually unpleasant month to be in Mumbai. While the rest of the country experiences autumnal bliss, Mumbai faces intense heat and humidity.

Unable to bear the heat, I did not leave the comfort of my air-conditioned house. My wife feared that I might turn into a recluse, and encouraged me to go out for business meetings, at least.

So when ACP Bopanna phoned and requested for a meeting, I was half inclined to accept it. But I had apprehensions about the matter he wanted to discuss with me. As such, I harboured a general dislike for the fellow. So I refused.

Mallya called afterwards and cajoled me to meet him. I fixed a meeting with Bopanna in the afternoon in a sports bar in Parel. I resolved to scrutinise two bundles of bank statements lying on my study table before going out to meet him.

I have my hands full these days. The reputation loss that my last employer Pharmabus had inflicted on me had been substantially attenuated by my fraud investigation into the affairs of Globosoft Chip Technologies Private Limited.

I managed to escape unscathed after Roopalaxmi's attempt on my life at the Hilton, but others were not so lucky. Building security had reacted in time, and a couple of security personnel had reached the floor by the time Puwaiya and I rushed out of my room. The ones who had reached the floor were unarmed.

When Roopalaxmi came out of the room in a fit, she fired indiscriminately, and wounded the housekeeping lady (the poor lady punctually serviced my floor that time of the day daily) and one security personnel, before she realised her folly and tried to run away. She had caused intense trauma to Hilton's guests who were too curious to remain in their respective rooms.

The police later arrested Roopalaxmi and her minions, and booked them for attempted murder and battery. Her real name was Aabidah Beevi, but she went by many aliases, and a thorough crackdown on her network revealed that she had multiple passports and identities.

When I showed the police the diary in my possession, and explained the terror financing scam I had uncovered, they handed the case to IB. Papers only reported a serious fraud at Globosoft that led to the murder of its MD by one of his employees. Officers from the Home Ministry and Prime Minister's Office interviewed me multiple times and appreciated my assistance in uncovering a major terror network.

I was handed a letter of appreciation, and an award on Independence Day. Saby Biswas spread the word in Mumbai that a new fraud detection specialist had emerged in the financial capital and I was swarmed with offers.

I took up a retainership with an audit firm's Fraud Investigation and Detection Service (FIDS) division. I was offered regular employment at an attractive salary, but was more inclined to start my own boutique. I took a small office space in Goregaon, to the East of the local station, and hired a single employee – Puwaiya. I gave a generous salary to relocate Puwaiya and his family. This arrangement suited his wife, who was fed up with his local friends in Bangalore.

I phoned Puwaiya and asked him to verify an address for me. I had found more than fifty companies operating from this single address. Eight of these fifty companies received funds from a Japanese MNC's India branch and immediately withdrew the money in cash. The Japanese promoters had hired me to find if the Indian managers were siphoning the branch's funds. I could crack the case if these fifty companies operating from the same address turned out to be shell companies.

I started for Parel in a cab after giving instructions to Puwaiya. I reached the bar to find Bopanna waiting for me. We shook hands and sat down. Bopanna was already having a beer. I ordered a cold drink and cheesy nachos.

Bopanna was apologetic about his conduct in relation to Globosoft. Without any instigation on my part, he gave a defence for his conduct.

He was not aware that Globosoft was a front for terror sympathisers. He always believed that it was a reputable corporate entity. He admitted that Anbu Selvam was giving him generous donations, which he claimed he needed to meet day-to-day running expenses of the station.

IB's investigation revealed an unusual involvement of Bopanna in activities of Globosoft. Based on their negative report, the state government had transferred him to faraway Bijapur district to manage a state reserve police force unit. I clarified to Bopanna that I had no role in that.

"So, Palani Kumar is not the man who stole forty crores?" Bopanna said.

"No. He was one of the fanatics bred to sacrifice himself for the cause. He committed suicide so as to put me off the scent I had picked up."

"Incredible," Bopanna whispered, more to himself. "Bala – real name Arif Aydeed – has confessed to police that Anbu committed suicide to implicate you. Is that true?"

The image of Anbu shooting himself came back to my mind. It still gave me shivers. I chose to remain silent, and Bopanna took the hint.

"Could you find out who took the money?" Bopanna asked.

I knew he would finally come to this question. *Yes, I have solved the case. I know who the Tourist is*. But I was not inclined to reveal this to Bopanna.

"No," I lied.

"Have you not wondered where all that money is lying?"

"It is beyond my brief. I was hired for a specific purpose. I fulfilled it and got my cheque."

"But you sure are curious, right? I mean, it's bad that someone swindled all that money."

"A tourist recruited Swati from Kathmandu. Surely you know that, right?"

Bopanna nodded.

"The Tourist and Swati stole blood money from a terrorist group. Blood money went from one group of criminals to another. Why would I care, unless I am an activist against black money?"

"The money went only to the Tourist," Bopanna said, "Swati is dead."

"What do you mean Swati is dead? You guys traced her IP location to Kuala Lumpur, right?"

"No. Someone had logged into her fake Facebook profile using mirror sites. We could not trace the source. I am guessing it was the Tourist, since Swati was long dead by then."

"Why do you think Swati was dead by then?"

"When I analysed her call records, I realised that she had gone to the Santacruz airport from Kalbadevi on 7 April. She met someone there. Then she went to Borivali. The trail vanishes after that. I employed a local police inspector here to painstakingly study all CCTV feeds in the airport area to find any clue. We saw from a feed of the taxi parking area that she picked up a lean and tall man wearing a pullover with a hood. His face was not visible. But the man was carrying a bag that had a picture of Mickey Mouse and other Disney characters on it.

"We studied footage of other CCTVs inside the airport and could get a capture of this man with his hood down. It took me quite some time to identify this man. The inspector found a criminal record against this man days after Roopalaxmi's arrest."

Bopanna took out a file and pulled out a photograph. It was a black & white photograph of a man coming out of an airport. He then pulled another photograph showing the same man standing outside a tea stall in a busy market.

"We do not know who this man is. In an unrelated investigation in Chandigarh, an engineer confessed to the police that he had hired a contract killer to eliminate his lover's husband. He had hired the contract killer over the internet, using the dark web. He had paid the contract killer in Bitcoins. Neither had he seen the contract killer, nor had the contract killer ever seen him. He had given a profile of the target and asked the contract killer for a quote. The contract killer gave a quote. The contract killer had good ratings from other users, which means that he could be trusted. The engineer paid 60% advance, after which the contract killer murdered the target. Then the engineer paid the balance amount.

"The case was never released to the media, because police feared that others may learn from the case and use the dark web to hire contract killers. What has the world come to? Drugs, body parts, women, all are being auctioned on the dark web. And now, contract killing?" Bopanna shook his head in trepidation.

"Who was the contract killer?"

"The police never found out. He is a phantom. But this picture shows the same man meeting the target in the Chandigarh case just before his death. The man was never identified. We do not know if this man was the contract killer. But it cannot be a mere coincidence.

"After Swati drugged Anbu, she took the ten rupees note, containing the Hawaladar's code, to Kalbadevi and exchanged it for eight bags of cash. Then she went to the airport and met this man. I am guessing that the Tourist had asked her to go to the airport and meet a person who would help her go back to Kathmandu. The Tourist had asked the contract killer to pose as that person and kill her. The contract killer took her to Borivali. My guess is, he disposed her SIM card in Borivali area, and drove her further outside the city. He killed her there and disposed of the body."

My head began to spin as I recalled Bidhya's clear inference that Swati was dead. My throat dried as I realised that I knew who the Tourist was, but had not done anything about it. A murderer was walking free, because I did not take my investigation to its logical conclusion.

"This contract killer, did you try to match his photo with your criminal record database using image processing software?" I asked.

"I have. This person does not have any criminal record."

I felt guilty. I was now half-inclined to share the Tourist's identity with Bopanna. But Bopanna spoiled his chances by saying that he was looking for the cash.

"I am sure Swati did not take the cash to the airport. The Tourist picked the cash from her in Kalbadevi, or on her way to the airport. Maybe the Hawaladar is the Tourist. The cash is most probably lying in India," Bopanna said. "If we partner, we can find the Tourist and the cash. Think about it! Forty crores shared fifty-fifty between us!"

"Why do you want a partner? Why don't you take hundred-hundred? Or will all your needs be quenched with twenty crores?"

"See, I am now in Bijapur. IB is keeping an eye on me. It's a bureaucratic post they have given me to manage training of a reserve police unit. It's difficult for me to get station leave. And you know the case well. We can work together. You identify the Tourist. Then I will bring my men and pick him up. We can interrogate him and find the cash," Bopanna said.

"Sorry, I am too busy. Find a partner whose disposition matches yours," I said and rose to leave. I took out some money, to which Bopanna protested, and left it on the table.

Once out of the bar, I phoned Biswas da, and asked his whereabouts. He was in Pharmabus office, but was not attending to any pressing matter. I asked him to meet me in an hour at the CCD outlet outside Pharmabus office, and took a cab.

I called Bidhya on the way to Pharmabus office. I admitted to her that she was probably right and Swati Gupta was dead. I regretted not taking her seriously earlier, and requested her to find the current circumstances of Swati's family.

▼

The dilemmas in the niche areas of corporate espionage and fraud detection are dense.

My role in Pharmabus was to provide critical insights into business and competitors to the company. The job involved collecting muck on competitors, studying their finances to give strategic directions to the company's management, and do all that is necessary to stay ahead of competition. I would spread disinformation about competitors so as to plateau their traded price on stock markets; leak information on their unethical deeds to the media; and question the deals they made with government officials.

My fellow accounts professionals at Pharmabus opened shell companies in tax havens to pay kickbacks for pharma licenses, purchased stolen formulas for medicines being researched by competitors, and developed complex structures to avoid paying taxes.

Are they right or wrong? When this is the norm in the industry, should an employee be faulted for following the employer's directions and facilitating bribe payments?

Because the boundaries are blurred, one suffers the risk of losing all sense of good and bad.

An informer tipped the management at Pharmabus that two of its competitors were selling spurious cancer drugs in African black market. A company willing to sell its drugs in a country needs a license from the drug control authority. The drug control authorities do not grant license if the drug has had negative results in clinical trials, or if it has side-effects. Many companies are not granted licenses because their product violates another company's product patent. Patents forbid other companies to replicate the drug's formulation for twenty years. Some companies without license still push their drugs in markets that have a high demand for the cure.

However, during my investigations in Nigeria, Kenya and Ghana, I found that Pharmabus itself was pushing spurious drugs into their black markets. It was clandestinely manufacturing three patented drugs – patented by a Canadian company – and pumping them into African black markets. Pharmabus had developed its version of the drugs which had remained untested.

It could not conduct clinical trials on broad populations legitimately, as it was copying another's patented product.

Without clinical trials on wide populations, you just cannot sell a drug. You do not know what side effects or fatalities the drug may cause. It will jeopardise the life of innocent patients.

But Pharmabus was doing exactly that. Its decade-long research into a new cancer product had not yielded any result. It was under immense pressure to recoup the research expenses. It decided to do so by pumping spurious drugs into African countries where citizens cannot afford costly patented drugs.

In an investigation ranging six months, I collected evidence that people were dying because of Pharmabus' drugs, and highlighted it to the management. The management refused to take any blame, and blamed me for doing my own investigations at the company's expense. I requested the management to stop selling the spurious drugs, a request they refused to acknowledge.

I was transferred to a division overseeing company audits. A vicious grapevine campaign was launched against me, questioning my loyalty to the company.

Undeterred, I wrote to health authorities in two of the African countries Pharmabus pumped its drugs in. The countries did not respond. Their bureaucracies, it seems, were too apathetic to respond. Then I did something that can be called 'crossing the line' in corporate espionage. I informed the Canadian company that owned the patent for the drug formulation. I shared the findings of my extensive research, hoping to mete justice on Pharmabus.

The Canadian company's lawyers confronted Pharmabus with the evidence. They had furtive internal discussions and struck a deal. Pharmabus paid a heavy compensation, in return for immunity from legal action. The payment was structured by one of my colleagues, and the overseas payment to the Canadian company was done by another. The Canadians disclosed to Pharmabus that I was their source.

I became an overnight pariah. I had committed the ultimate act of dishonesty in corporate espionage: while I was supposed to collect intel on competitors for my employer, I collected intel on my employer for its competitors. I had double-crossed my employer. Some colleagues whispered around that I had made good money for myself by selling information to the Canadians, even though that was a complete lie.

It is easy to draw an ethical line, but difficult to stand by it. Consequences can be career-damaging for someone in fraud detection. I had drawn my line. I would not compromise on an innocent's life. It kept me away from darkness. But it also had grave consequences for my career. I was fired on a flimsy charge. My employer gave especially vicious feedback about me to anyone who was considering me for a job.

These are consequences that I had not comprehended when I decided to be the hero.

I had almost decided to change my line of work, and start statutory audit from scratch, when Globosoft happened. I now had a reputation and a fresh start with FIDS.

Unfortunately, the ethical dilemmas in FIDS are not any simpler. I had to confide what I knew with someone. I decided that there was no one better to reach out for advice than my mentor at Pharmabus, Saby Biswas.

19

The Right Thing

Saby Biswas was curious about the identity of the Tourist since the day I had narrated to him how I unearthed an underground network of terror financiers while investigating Swati Gupta. He guessed over a long evening of drinks that I probably knew who the Tourist was.

"You are not the type to leave a mystery alone. You are more the type who would climb a difficult peak because it exists."

"Well, yes I had figured out the real Tourist," I said.

"So you came rushing to reveal to me who this Tourist is?" Biswas da asked as we settled with cappuccino and garlic bread slices.

"Yes. I always thought that the tourist and Swati Gupta had together swindled the terror financiers' money. After all, forty crores are enough for them to share. But a policeman who was investigating the case for Globosoft showed me proof that the Tourist hired a contract killer to eliminate Swati," I said.

"If you remember, I had told you that Swati was dead?' Biswas da said.

'Yes and Bidhya, the journalist I hired in Kathmandu to look into her family, also told me the same thing. But I did not think the Tourist is capable of committing murder. He turns out to be much more devious than I thought."

"So who is the Tourist?"

"Deepak Bhide, the guy who hired me."

"Seriously? The dimwit Swati took as her husband."

"That is his strength. No one in Globosoft doubted him. No one was looking his way. He never made it to the suspect list because of his pretence."

"But you know him since college, right?"

"I never really knew him in college. He was not a part of my circle, nor Nidhi's. He was good in mathematics and computers, but socially awkward. My friends made fun of him. My perception of Bhide was based on these biases. As it turns out, he is an evil mastermind," I chuckled and took a sip of coffee.

"So he brought Swati Gupta to India, and prepared her for the heist?"

"Yep."

"And he hired you also?"

"Yes. Try to understand his modus operandi, and it will impress you. He maintained the company's accounts on SAP. He noted that the Malabar Children Education Society was bringing about a hundred crores from abroad and distributing the money among shady NGOs in south India. And then the funds stopped. He guessed that Selvam was bringing in the money through an alternate route.

"Bhide was close to Selvam. He snooped on him and found out that Selvam was bringing the donations through the Hawala route and utilising it here in India. What he was doing was clearly illegal. So, if some of this money got stolen, Selvam would not file a police complaint. He would use private goons to search for the thief. If the thief vanishes into thin air, Selvam would meet a dead-end. He would not, in any case, tip the police… for he would risk getting himself exposed.

"Bhide hatched a plan. He needed someone dispensable to gain Selvam's confidence and track his activities. Basically, a mistress for Selvam. When the Hawala money comes, the mistress has to get the ten rupees note containing the Hawaladar's code and pick the cash. The mistress has to be eliminated after the heist, because Selvam would be searching her. She is a loose end he could not afford to leave unattended.

"But her family would file a police complaint, and that may lead the police to Bhide. So he decided to get a woman from Nepal for the job. He rummaged through the prostitution networks in Kathmandu and paid sex workers for a night's service. He spoke with these women and gauged their level of desperation. He sensed in Preeti Gurung – that's Swati's real name – an aspiration to get out of the cycle of impoverishment she was in. Being in the call girl business, she was also skilled enough to lure an immoral man.

"Bhide brought her to India and trained her. He introduced her to his colleagues and his boss as his wife. Swati used this access to seduce Selvam, and became his mistress. She slept with Selvam and snooped into his smartphone chats. Selvam must have communicated the number code on a ten-rupee note to a Hawaladar in Mauritius. This Hawaladar sent the money to

Kedia, his partner Hawaladar in Mumbai. Swati found out about this consignment from Selvam's smartphone.

"Anbu Selvam and Palani Kumar worked independently. They both reported to Roopalaxmi. Selvam was charged with maintaining accounts. That's why he maintained a diary containing details of offshore banks from which funds came, and beneficiaries to whom the funds were paid. He also possessed the ten rupees note that had to be produced to take delivery of cash from the Hawaladar.

"Palani controlled the musclemen. He sent the men who would pick cash from the Hawaladar and safely carry the cash to various destinations in Tamil Nadu and Karnataka.

"Swati drugged Selvam on 7 April and took the note containing Kedia's code. Palani had sent his men to pick the note from Selvam. They were calling him, but could not reach him. So Palani phoned Swati multiple times that morning, asking for his whereabouts. She used some excuse to deflect his questions. She reached Kedia's office and produced the ten rupee note. The Hawaladar handed eight bags of cash to her, which she kept in a safe place in Kalbadevi itself – on Bhide's instructions.

"Bhide had parallelly hired a contract killer on the dark web, by paying in Bitcoins. He had given Swati's number to the contract killer – through Silk Route's messaging service, I am guessing, and a pseudonym he can go by. He asked Swati to meet the contract killer at the airport. He probably told Swati that the stranger at the airport would take her to safety till matters cooled.

"The killer murdered Swati and disposed of her body at a place from where it has still not been found. And no one is looking. Her family in Kathmandu filed a police complaint there. The station has to fulfil enormous formalities and prepare arduous paperwork in order to request Indian authorities to investigate the matter. They wouldn't do this for a lone case, especially if the victim is a nobody. More than ten thousand Nepali women are trafficked to India every year. I am guessing the number of missing women cases that the police in Nepal has to deal with are staggering.

"Bhide's plan worked smoothly till now. He remained in the shadows. His awkward demeanour and comical look made him an object of pity and ridicule. Palani and his goons did not suspect him even a bit. They did not even extract his phone records. He was an outlier in their list of suspects.

"But Palani kept digging. The amount involved was huge, and Roopalaxmi showed personal interest in the investigation. They were afraid that someone knew about their little secret. Bhide had not expected that Palani and his team would keep investigating for so long.

"This spooked Bhide. Bhide panicked when he found from Palani that his team was searching for an elusive Tourist who recruited Swati, in Kathmandu. His chances of getting exposed increased with each passing day. To stop them, he used two strategies.

"First, he hired me. He even told me a cock-and-bull story on how he was raped by two gay perverts, to reinforce my bias that he is a chutiya – an idiot. It must have taken him a long time to find the right man for the job. He needed someone who could dig into the company's secrets, and ask uncomfortable questions. I am a certified forensic auditor. And I was unemployed at the time.

"To be frank to you, I did not do anything extraordinary. But the villains got nervous when I seized Selvam's diary containing their shadow accounts. They behaved just the way Bhide had expected them to behave.

"His second strategy was to send them on the wrong trail. He logged into Swati's fake FB profile from a mirror site in Kuala Lumpur to divert their attention from Kathmandu. As he had wanted, Palani's team diverted their energy towards searching for Swati in Kuala Lumpur."

"What made you suspect Bhide?" Biswas da asked.

"I met Bhide's therapist on my last day in Bangalore. Nidhi was worried that Bhide was losing his mind after Palani committed suicide – the bastard acted so well that I was also convinced. I had promised Nidhi that I would arrange for his therapy before leaving Bangalore. When I finally met the therapist, he told me that Bhide was never a regular client. He visited the doctor a couple of times, but discontinued thereafter.

"This made me suspicious. I bribed an attendant at the clinic and got Bhide's case history. It said that Bhide had a low self-esteem and was overly conscious about his looks. Some colleagues at office made fun of him and called him names, which hurt him. This triggered a visit to the therapist.

"The therapist's own conclusion was that Bhide was not suffering from depression. He had a low self-esteem, which could be addressed through Rogerian therapy and positive regard. Bhide attended just three therapy sessions three years back.'

"I guess he got back at his colleagues by stealing from them," Biswas da quipped.

"This got me suspicious. Why would Bhide lie about his therapist? People who seek a shrink's help generally hide it. Why would Bhide lie that he consulted a therapist when actually he did not? My understanding that Bhide *could* lie changed everything. He was not an innocent simpleton after all. He was as complex as anyone else. This put him in my suspects list. I realised that he was my number one suspect after I put him in the list."

"How did he become your top suspect?"

"I did a thought experiment. I placed him in the position of the Tourist and simulated the events. Things fit in. In the right kind of game, the Tourist will have the maximum payoff from the events that unfurled. I found what economists call an equilibrium situation when I made Bhide the Tourist. His payoff was the maximum from the events that followed."

"You used game theory? My god, Digyen!"

"But I was still not sure. Bhide did not look like the type who would pull off something this big. No criminal record, no history of felony, and he goes on to pull off a master heist single-handedly? I recalled how sharp he was in mathematics and computer programming. But that was not enough proof. So I requested the IB guys I had befriended after exposing Globosoft's underground network for Bhide's call detail records.

"They gave me his call records for the last four years. It was a trove of information. He has left the country approximately in the periods in which the Tourist met Swati in Kathmandu and recruited her. His last tower location before leaving India each time is near Ghaziabad. Ghaziabad is near the Sunauli border between India and Nepal. Ghaziabad does not have any international airport to take Bhide to some other country. So I concluded that he had gone to Nepal each of these times he left the country. He went to Nepal through the land borders, so as not to leave any trace.

"Bhide had gone to Mumbai on 31 March. Swati duped Anbu Selvam on 7 April. What was Bhide doing on 31 March? Bhide is a Maharashtrian. His parents are based in a suburb in Vashi, which is in Navi Mumbai. Bhide landed in Mumbai early in the morning and went straight to Dadar. He stayed there for the entire day, and returned to Bangalore early next morning. What was he doing in Dadar? Why did he not visit his parents while he was in Mumbai?

"Bhide has revisited Dadar three times after Swati's disappearance. He takes a morning flight, goes to Dadar, and comes back to the airport. He did not meet his parents in either of these times.'

"So the cash is in a bank locker in Dadar?"

"Which bank will give you a locker big enough to keep eight bags of cash? Forty crores is a lot of money. Big bank branches keep it in their strong rooms."

"So?"

"My guess is that he has rented a flat. Dadar is just twenty minutes away from Kalbadevi, and is situated on the way to the airport at Santacruz. He rented a flat there and gave a key to Swati. Swati picked eight bags of cash from Kalbadevi and dropped them in this flat on her way to the airport."

"Wow!" Biswas da exclaimed, "This guy is a genius."

"I wanted to test my hypothesis. So I raised a trumped up bill for my services to him. I was in Bangalore for ten odd days. I billed Bhide five thousand rupees per hour for 250 work hours which comes to 12.50 lakhs. Add to that my travel and stay expenses, and a generous compensation for Puwaiya for a month. I expected Bhide to bargain with me, or request me to reduce the per hour rate. He did not. He transferred the money in full. Just that, the money did not come from his account. Rather, it came from a *jan dhan* account. I am sure he made a cash deposit in the account and transferred the money to me."

"And then?" Biswas da asked me when I fell silent.

"I did not pursue the matter any further. I have not revealed to anyone else that I know the truth about Bhide. I could have sent a message across to Roopalaxmi informing her who the real Tourist is. I did not. Did I do the right thing?" I said.

"Your client hired you to provide him services. You did that. Going beyond the mandate violates the code of conduct of this profession. You did the right thing. It's professionalism."

"Is it still professionalism to maintain confidentiality now, after getting to know that Bhide murdered Swati?"

"That's a conjecture made by a policeman. It is the police's duty to book murderers. Why should you get involved in it?"

"But the policeman is not doing his duty. He is sniffing around for the bounty," I said.

"So what? This is an imperfect world. It is unethical of the policeman to not perform his duty. You cannot randomly do his *dharma*. You have your own dharma, which is the code of conduct of your profession."

I did not understand what I had expected to hear from Biswas da. I was disappointed with him, but could not reject his point of view.

"You think I was wrong when I blew the whistle on Pharmabus?"

"I am personally glad you did that. The company was killing patients in Africa. It learnt its lesson when it had to pay a large compensation to the patent owner. After you left, the company also had to pay off some drug control authorities in Africa you had complained to."

"But?"

"I am still working in the company. Knowing very well that Pharmabus has indulged in immoral activities, I still draw my pay from it," Biswas da said.

"I have been in this profession for many more years than you, Digyen. I can tell you, most companies transgress the words of law. Law itself is so stringent and overbearing that you cannot do business and follow the word of law at the same time. Where should I draw the line? I will work for this company, but not that company... where will this lead me?"

"So you think it was wrong of me to blow the whistle?"

"*Yes!* You violated the trust that our management reposed on you. The management was engaged in illegal and immoral activities, not you. They did not ask anything immoral of you. They gave you a job. The professional thing to do here is to do your job. You found muck about the company, by virtue of your position in the company, and you splashed it around."

"So what do I do with the realisation that Bhide is a murderer?"

"Keep it close to your heart. It will make for a great story to tell in parties and get-togethers. You have learnt this not in your capacity as a citizen, but in your capacity as a professional hired by Bhide. You owe the confidentiality to him."

▼

I took out a photograph of Swati on the drive back home, and stared at her eyes. She looked like a kind person, just like my wife. She had innocent eyes. She got into prostitution to pay for her father's medicines. Trading her body for subsistence is never easy for a woman.

Swati left a toddler and came to India to participate in Bhide's devious plan. Her heart must have bled. But she did what she had to do, to secure the future of her children.

To hell with professionalism! I will do the right thing and save my soul.

20

The Game Plan

I had a game plan ready by the time Sneha came back from office. She served dinner, while I narrated the entire story to her. She had her apprehensions about my plan, but could not come up with a better one.

I had a video chat with Bidhya in the morning, in which she informed me that Swati's father had passed away two weeks back. The orphaned kids were under the care of a cousin of Swati's in the same slum.

I offered to send one lakh rupees immediately for their welfare, and promised more in coming days. I told Bidhya that Bhide was the mysterious Tourist and asked her to take Bhide's photograph and ID proof and conduct another enquiry in the area around the Knight Rider bar. Bhide has such jocular features that any waiter who has served him in a dance bar would remember him. With his short height and immature looks, he would look like a child in a dance bar.

I also asked her to inform the local police station that Preeti Gurung alias Swati Gupta was last seen with her lover Deepak

Bhide in Bangalore. They should prepare the paperwork and send a letter rogatory through their embassy to a court in Bangalore for investigation on human trafficking.

I ended my video call with Bidhya and went to the Air India building on Marine Drive. This building hosts the investigation wing of Mumbai's income tax department.

I went to the Director General's office and asked for the person handling informers. I was directed to an ITO. The ITO took what appeared like hours to fill archaic forms and gave me an informer code. I could approach any sleuth working in the investigation wing using the code.

I asked the ITO which officer I should approach if I have intel on a cash hoard. He laughed and informed me that such information usually turns out to be incorrect. Many citizens who turn informers for the department try to use the department to settle scores with business rivals by claiming that their rivals sit on hoards of cash. So, senior officers avoid such informers. I would have more luck with a junior officer.

I went through the list of officers and selected Smita Shinde, an IRS officer, and requested an appointment through the ITO. The directorate of investigation is generally dominated by male officers, who bond well and hunt in packs.

Female officers who make it to the investigation wing often burn with a desire to outperform 'the boys' and prove themselves. I had a better chance with Smita Shinde than any male officer.

True to my prediction, Smita Shinde called me into her chamber in an instant and asked me about my intel. Rather than hooting about cash stashes, which every other informer must be doing, I decided to narrate her the story.

I told her about Hawaladar Ramakrishna Kedia, and how he brought forty crores of cash to fund training centres of a radicalisation group in south India; how the money never reached the beneficiaries and is now lying in a flat in Dadar. And how a raid on the Hawaladar will reveal many other transactions in black money.

"What about the cash?" Smita asked.

"The cash is lying in a flat in Dadar. I have identified the person who possesses the cash. But I have not managed to identify the flat," I said.

"We can put a surveillance on this person," Smita said.

"Good idea. But he won't discuss the cash and its whereabouts with anyone. We need to catch him when he goes to the flat," I said.

"So we maintain surveillance till he goes to the flat? What if he does not go to the flat for months?"

"Leave that to me. I will make him go to the flat. You have to track his every movement using triangulation technology. Can you do that?"

Triangulation is the process of determining the exact geographical location of a mobile phone. It is a sure shot way of tracking a person's movements. Smita nodded, indicating that triangulation will not be a problem for her.

"Now coming to the main issue – how can I trust you?" Smita asked.

"You should *not* trust me. I am a walk-in informer. Why should you?" I said.

Smita smiled and said, "I do not have powers to issue warrants. I have to convince my Director Investigation for a warrant. If I get a warrant, I have to show results. I cannot go around the city violating personal rights of citizens on the basis of mere claims."

"Fair enough! You can check the credibility of my intel by conducting a small inspection at the office of Hawaladar Kedia. As regards the cash, it's a once-in-a-career intel for you. You do not lose anything if you do not find any cash. You don't have to execute the warrant. But if you do find forty crore rupees in pink notes, it will be the biggest seizure in your office for a long time to come."

I could see the spark in her eyes that came from a hunger to prove herself in the male-dominated directorate. She might even jump into a well if I tell her that a few kilograms of gold are hidden in it.

"I am a qualified chartered accountant. I won't waste my time on this treasure hunt if I wasn't sure about it. My self-interest is involved here. By the way, how much will be my reward?"

"It's a complex formula we use; reward could be from 1% to 10% of the amount found, subject to a maximum of 5 crore rupees."

"Wow. You guys are incentivising the next generation of bounty hunters! No wonder so many shady characters have made a profession out of supplying information to the department."

I shared Bhide's number, photograph and other details with Smita.

I requested her to conduct an inspection in the Hawaladar's office and give it wide coverage in newspapers. I convinced her that it was important for her to investigate the Hawaladar, so that I could lay my trap.

▼

Smita stuck to her end of the bargain and conducted a tax survey on Kediaji's office in Kalbadevi. Her team found eighty lakh rupees in his dingy office, but the real trove was the whatsApp chats with his customers on transactions in crores of rupees. She executed a warrant and seized the cash and digital evidence. Then, she leaked details of the raid to the media. On my request, she gave a byte to beat reporters that Kediaji used GPS technology to track the movement of cash after customers picked their money. The news was flashed in many local newspapers, and a few national newspapers as well.

The minor success increased Smita's confidence on my intel. She was now ready for the big haul.

21

The Final Act

The final act was an anti-climax of sorts – it unravelled as I had plotted.

IT raids on Kedia alarmed Bhide. Although it was weird for a Hawaladar to track cash bags through GPS tracking chips, Bhide did not want to take any chance. He reached Mumbai just two days after the IT raids on Kediaji got flashed in newspapers.

It was a Sunday. Smita's team was not ready for this. Luckily, a technical expert in the department's computer forensics lab noted Bhide's arrival in Mumbai from the triangulation software and intimated her. She spoke with her boss and mobilised a team of four inspectors and an ITO. She managed to requisition an escort vehicle with four armed constables from the police commissioner's office.

Bhide had reached Dadar by the time Smita mobilised the team. The technical guy identified his location as an upscale apartment complex in Dadar East. I started for the location immediately after getting location specifics from Smita.

Smita's team moved swiftly and took the gate security of the apartment complex into control. They checked the in-out register and found that Bhide had entered the apartment complex twenty minutes before them. He had rented a flat on the third floor.

One inspector went to the tower's backside to keep an eye on the flat's balcony. Another took control of the reception. Smita picked up the receptionist as a witness and entered the lift with her team.

Smita pressed the doorbell outside Bhide's flat and waited for a response. Smita had to press the bell a few more times before Bhide answered. He shouted out to her from the other side, asking her about her identity. Smita said in Marathi that she is from the building maintenance and has to take his signature on some documents. Bhide said from inside that he would come down to the maintenance room and sign the documents.

Smita insisted that she has to get his signature immediately since it was a Sunday and she had to go early. She complained how he was hard to reach. Bhide opened the door reluctantly, and found a smart girl in boy-cut hairstyle smiling at him. Smita's team barged into the flat before Bhide could react.

They found thirty-eight crores and twenty lakhs in pink notes inside Bhide's flat. And thus, Smita registered the biggest cash seizure in Mumbai that year. Bhide was caught transferring the cash from old bags to new bags.

Suspicious about the source of this cash, the department informed Director of Enforcement (ED) about possible money laundering. ED prepared a prima facie case and took Bhide into temporary custody. Later, Kedia confessed that he had facilitated the transfer of this cash from tax havens through the Hawala route. The income tax department initiated prosecution under a draconian law called the Black Money Act. It froze his life's savings, on the pretext that the tax plus interest plus penalty will be more than the amount seized.

Bhide's parents managed to get him out on bail after a month. But he was in a sorry state. Saddled with multiple cases from multiple agencies, he now faced fresh investigations from Nepali authorities on charges of trafficking Swati into India and allegedly selling her into slavery.

I watched the plot unfold from the shadows. I got a sizable reward from the department, which I shared with the NGO taking care of Swati's children. The income tax department follows stringent informer protection policy, due to which Bhide did not know that I was the mind behind his downfall. He would eventually find out, I being the boast I am.

But I was not over with Bhide yet. He had murdered an innocent woman, after all. He has to live in fear, for the rest of his pathetic life.

I got a new SIM card under a fictitious name a few days after Bhide was out on bail and sent him a message.

You stole our money. We are coming for you!

List of Acronyms

ACP – Assistant Commissioner of Police
CDR – Call Detail Record
CP – Commissioner of Police
DG – Director General
ED – Enforcement Directorate
FATF – Financial Action Task Force
FCRA – Foreign contribution regulation Act
FIDS – Fraud Investigation and Detection Service
FIR – First Information Report
GPS – Global Positioning System
IB – Intelligence Bureau
IRS – Indian Revenue Services
ITO – Income Tax Office
KIADB – Karnataka Industrial Areas Development Board
MD – Managing Director
NGO – Non-governmental Organisation
PE – Private Equity
SHO – Station House Officer